To Sister Taylor

Best wishes for your retirement.

Love from

Janet

THE LOVE THEY
ONCE SHARED

"I don't deserve to live!" The girl's despairing cry, heard above the crashing of the waves, haunted Charlotte Saunders. What was the tragedy the young girl could not forget? Did her future really lie with the husband who had hurt her so deeply? Where had her Aunt Rose, the one person she felt could help her, vanished to?

Charlotte had come home to Baynton to help her friend, Margaret Gregson. Now the girl's troubles, and the need Charlotte felt to help her, widened the rift between Charlotte and her friend, Bill Menzies. Would the rift heal? Or would the return of Margaret's son, Charlotte's childhood sweetheart, from America, widen it still further?

As Charlotte fought other people's battles, she found herself in danger of losing her own happiness.

THE LOVE THEY ONCE SHARED

RAINBOW
ROMANCE

Mary Ledgway Temple

ROBERT HALE · LONDON

ISBN 0 7090 4149 7

Robert Hale Limited
Clerkenwell House
Clerkenwell Green
London EC1R 0HT

For a dear son, Peter

Photoset by Saxon Printing Ltd., Derby.
Printed and bound by Interprint Ltd.,
Valletta, Malta.

One

The boy and girl walked slowly, quietly, along the cliffs. Normally they ran, racing each other along the rough path, scrambling over the rocky parts. Normally they called to each other, laughing, teasing. Or rather the boy teased; the girl was quieter, hiding the hurt she sometimes felt.

Patchy mist whirled round them. Except for the screeching of the gulls, they were in a world of their own. Huge, white topped waves dashed over the pebbly beach far below. Looking down, the girl shivered.

This was not lost upon the boy. Although he was thirteen years old to her eleven, he was a good two inches shorter. Suddenly he felt that today of all days he had to show his superiority.

He was carrying a ball, a red leather ball, a special ball, a present, something he had long coveted. He made to pass it to the girl, but he fumbled and the ball rolled over the edge of the cliff.

As though aiding and abetting the boy, the mist rolled away. They stood looking down at the splash of red on the sand.

5

'I can't lose it – it's new,' the boy said abruptly. 'It was your fault. You'll have to go down and get it.'

They both knew it wasn't the girl's fault and the boy also knew that the thought of going down the treacherous cliff filled her with terror. He wanted her to refuse – to admit fear, but that was something she had never done.

The girl looked at the ball, remembering how expensive it had been. Remembering, too, how she had pleaded with her mother, trying to explain how much the gift mattered. Now it was far below on the sands – and already the waves were creeping nearer.

The girl moved towards the path. The boy stood back to let her pass. Their eyes met. For an instant he saw the fear and almost relented. But she had to be the first one to back down; she had to be.

She took the first hesitant steps towards the worn track. The wind blew her hair so that she had to shake it out of her eyes. Her feet, clad only in worn sandals slipped on the loose surface and she fell on her knees as she searched for further footholds.

A curtain of mist rolled in from the sea and she was lost to sight. When it cleared she had reached the sands and was running towards the ball. Holding it to her, she turned and looked up at the boy on the cliff.

The sea was already washing the headland. She knew she would never be able to climb back up the path. There were few handholds to pull herself up and the rain mist, heavier now, made the narrow, stony track almost impassable.

The boy called out to her, but the wind and sea tossed away his words. She stood motionless, paralysed.

Another sweep of mist rolled in from the sea, then rolled away. When it cleared the boy was no longer there. Despair racked her.

Then she saw him scrambling down. He moved quickly and was soon beside her.

'Here! Give me that!' He took the ball, stuffing it inside his jacket. 'The path from the next bay is easier. Come on!'

'No, I can't—'

But he took her hand and dragged her behind him. The waves reached past their knees, the spray soaked them but still he pressed on, gripping her so hard his fingers dug into her flesh.

Only when they were in the next bay did he give her a moment to regain her breath. Then he urged her to the foot of the cliffs.

'You go first. It's an easier climb than the other.'

He pushed her in front of him. She tried to help herself by pulling on the short tufts of grass, and the occasional outcrop of sandy stone. Twice the grass gave way and they slithered back.

At last they were at the top. With one final burst of strength they heaved themselves over the edge, sprawling full length onto the sparse turf, both too exhausted to speak.

After a few minutes they sat up eyeing each other. The girl didn't ask why he had let her take the hardest path – and he didn't say sorry. It was not their way.

Instead he reached out a hand and touched her wet jacket.

'We must go back. Get dry.'

They rose slowly, reluctantly. The boy unzipped his jacket and forced the ball into the safety of a pocket.

'I'll always keep it,' he told her. 'Always!'

Their eyes went back down to the sea. Not even a small strip of sand was visible now. Waves crashed angrily against the cliffs.

Both children shivered. In an unaccustomed gesture the boy took the girl's hand as they turned away.

As though tired of playing tricks, the sun came out and the rain clouds rolled away. Their steps slowed.

But all too soon they were at the end of an avenue of houses. Large houses, set well back from the tree-lined road. This was where the boy lived.

'I don't want to go,' he said with sudden urgency. 'But I have to. Dad says he can't turn the job down.

'Seven years will soon pass and then we'll be back. We're letting the house furnished so we will be coming back here to live. We'll still be friends – we'll always be friends.'

The girl nodded and he released her hand. She watched him walk slowly away; watched him turn and raise a hand in farewell. Then she was alone.

There was no need now to check the threatening tears. Seven years stretched out in front of her like an eternity. The boy would have new surroundings, new friends; life in New York would be exciting. The thought that he might forget her, that she might never see him again, filled her with dread – .

Her steps were slow as she walked the rest of the way to the small terrace house that was her home. Her mother looked at her tear-stained face and opened her arms.

'There, love. Don't fret yourself.'

Characteristically her mother did not scold her for the torn skirt and the wet clothes. Gently she stroked the damp, tangled hair and gradually the girl grew calmer.

'There, lassie. Go and get out of those wet clothes. I've made pan muffins for tea. We'll eat nice and cosy round the fire.'

The girl, warm now, safe and loved in her own home, smiled as she went up the narrow stairs. Nothing could hurt her now.

Two

Charlotte Saunders had just finished her evening meal when the telephone rang. Bill, she thought, a warm glow enveloping her. But it wasn't Bill. It was Doctor Wade, speaking from her home town of Baynton. Charlotte listened with growing dismay.

'How ill is she, Doctor?'

'It's hard to say, my dear. But I think she should go into hospital. Unfortunately she is equally certain it is not necessary, and you know what a stubborn lady Margaret Gregson is! She just won't listen to me.'

'Are you saying I ought to come home?'

'No – no, my dear! Just suggesting.' The old doctor spoke with his customary courtesy. 'There doesn't seem to be anyone else.'

Charlotte laid the receiver down and went into her small kitchen to reheat her coffee. Her actions were mechanical, her thoughts troubled.

Doctor Wade was right. There was no-one else. Margaret Gregson was an unusually private person. Charlotte knew she was one of the few people the older woman counted among her friends. Charlotte had become very fond of Margaret after she had proved herself such a good friend to her mother, during Emma Saunders' last brief illness.

Her mind was already made up. Today was Thursday. On Saturday she would travel home to Yorkshire and to Baynton.

Getting time off from the health clinic where she worked would be easy. Charlotte had filled in for members of the staff during a flu epidemic, and not only had time off due to her, but holidays as well. But there was Bill Menzies to think of.

She glanced at the clock. Dare she ring him?

She knew he would be in his flat, working on plans for some gardens he had been commissioned to design and she didn't want to disturb him. He was still on the bottom rung of the ladder after completing his studies as a landscape gardener. No – she would wait until their date tomorrow evening.

Charlotte sipped her coffee and glanced round her attic flat. It was only a few minutes walk from the health centre and convenient for shopping and the Tube station when she needed it.

The dormer windows looked over the rooftops of the North London suburb. Inside, white paint and bright covers had transformed dull rooms into a comfortable place to live.

Charlotte liked her work, and her surroundings. She felt a sudden foreboding as she thought of the journey on Saturday. It was quite a while since she had visited Baynton.

Bill had reserved a table at a small hotel, and drove confidently through the heavy traffic. The April eve-

11

ning was warm and they felt a quiet contentment in each other's company. Neither felt a need to talk.

It was not until they had finished their meal that Charlotte told Bill about her impending visit to Baynton.

'I'm sorry, Bill, but Mrs Gregson is rather special to me. She's a good friend. I know Doctor Wade wouldn't have rung me without thinking about it carefully. If I didn't go and anything happened. . . .'

Bill Menzies smiled ruefully.

'I know! It's just that, well—'

Just that I don't want you to go, he thought. But he didn't dare say it. He had known Charlotte for only three weeks, and, a quiet, shy man he was afraid to say anything that might jeopardise their friendship. Instead he leaned over the table.

'Gregson? Isn't that the name of that boy you used to play with? The one who has gone back to America?'

'Yes! He may have to come home. I'll wait to see how things are.'

Charlotte, bending to retrieve a fallen napkin didn't see the shadow cross Bill's face. When he stood up and suggested a walk in the grounds before their coffee, she agreed with a smile.

'Oh, this is heavenly,' she told him as they walked by a shallow lake, bordered by tulips, daffodils and hyacinths. Charlotte breathed deeply, drinking in the sweet smelling air.

'A real breath of spring, in a London garden. I think spring flowers are the loveliest of all. They hold so much promise.'

It wasn't late when Bill dropped her at her flat. Charlotte had intended asking him in for coffee, instead she smiled her thanks.

'Good night, Bill. I have an early start in the morning. It's been a lovely evening.'

He took her hands, looking down at her in the half light.

'I'm sorry I can't come to the station, but I have quite a drive out to Chanlea for my appointment. It's my biggest commission yet – about six acres – and I want to make a success of it. I think the owner should like my sketches, but you can never be sure,' he finished ruefully.

'He'll be a fool if he doesn't. I love your landscaping ideas. The ones you've shown me, anyway.'

He reached out and touched her hair, letting his fingers trail until they were tilting her face to his.

'You will come back to London?'

'Oh, yes! I'll come back.'

For a brief moment Charlotte held her breath. Was he going to kiss her? The moment passed, and he dropped her hands.

'Take care of yourself,' Bill said softly. 'Have a safe journey. I hope your friend isn't too ill.'

Charlotte stood inside the open door watching him drive away. She had been out with other men, but somehow, Bill Menzies seemed different. She hoped he was not walking out of her life for long.

King's Cross Station was busy, the train crowded. She managed to find a seat and as her journey began, she found herself looking back.

Inevitably, knowing she would soon be seeing his mother, her thoughts turned to Derek Gregson. She remembered the day he had left for America – and her wild delight when she heard he was bringing his mother home to Baynton.

Derek's father had collapsed just before his seven years in America were completed. Although Derek had wanted to stay in America he had yielded to his mother's pleading and returned to Yorkshire.

The months that followed had held a magical quality for Charlotte, but, all too soon she was saying good-bye again.

This time she waved Derek off from the airport, with Margaret Gregson by her side. Somehow she put aside her own distress to help the older woman come to terms with parting from her son.

Idly, Charlotte's mind registered the changing countryside. The flat green fields began to undulate, and there were glimpses of rivers glinting in the sun. She went up to the buffet car and bought tea and a toasted sandwich. By the time she had eaten it they were in Yorkshire, passing through the small, neglected stations that had always saddened her mother.

Emma Saunders had loved to tell her daughter about the country stations of the old days. Days when the porters, or any of the station staff would fill their spare time in working on the patches of garden in their station. Emma would describe the cosy waiting rooms, many of them proudly displaying a 'Best-kept Station' certificate. Now the platforms were weed-ridden, the waiting rooms vandalised and locked.

But the rolling hills and woodlands were as beauti-ful as ever and Charlotte leaned forward eagerly to catch the first glimpse of York. She loved the town, it always made her feel she was nearly home.

There was little time to spare as she hurried over the

old iron bridge at York Station. The Scarborough train was already in and Charlotte smiled gratefully at the young child who clambered onto her mother's knee, to allow her to sit down.

The child was a little chatterbox and, in spite of her mother's half-hearted protests, insisted on showing 'the lady' her books. Charlotte, fond of children didn't mind. In fact she was grateful to the little girl for taking her mind off her problems.

Charlotte hurried to the bus station and found a bus to Baynton was just about to pull out. It was half empty and as she climbed aboard she looked round, wondering if she would see a familiar face.

The passengers were all strangers, mostly elderly. The only young person on the bus was a girl in a red jacket, sitting on the opposite side.

The first thing Charlotte noticed about her was her hair, gloriously auburn, curly. How sad, thought Charlotte, that she doesn't take more care. The hair was dull, lifeless and what Charlotte could see of the girl's face was pale, only her lips moved as she moistened them. They must be dry, Charlotte thought. Was she ill?

The half hour ride was soon over and they were at Charlotte's stop. As she stood up, her movements disturbed the girl in the red jacket. She rose, too, her movements jerky, as though suddenly aroused from sleep.

Charlotte stood back to let the stranger alight first, but halfway down the steps she suddenly turned back.

'Steady on there!' the driver cautioned. 'Let the lady off.'

The strap of the girl's shoulder bag had caught on the rail, checking the girl's movements. Charlotte leaned over, helping her to release it, and the girl gave her a quick look. Her lips formed a word or two, but her voice was low and Charlotte wasn't sure whether she was thanking her for her help or apologising for her bad manners.

Charlotte stood, watching the bus drive away, then she turned and walked the short distance to her little terrace home. Soon her own problems had driven all thoughts of the girl in the red jacket from her mind.

Pausing only to wash her hands and face, Charlotte rang the doctor's surgery.

'Oh, it's you, Charlotte!' The receptionist greeted her warmly.

'Beryl! You're still there then. Can I see Doctor Wade today?'

'Actually, he half expected you. He has only one more patient to see, so come now.'

Charlotte felt some of her depression lift as she listened to Beryl. Beryl Masters, or Burton as she was now, had been at school with Charlotte. Against her parents' wishes she had married young, but it seemed she was still in her old job.

But not for much longer, Charlotte thought as Beryl greeted her.

'Marriage is suiting you,' she told her.

The young wife laughed, patting the bulge under her loose smock.

'I can recommend it any time! Even Mum and Dad are on our side now. Anyway the doctor is ready, so go straight in.'

Dr Wade motioned Charlotte to take a seat and

nodded to Beryl.

'Coffee please, Beryl – then you can go. Good girl that. I'll be sorry to lose her.'

Charlotte nodded, then came straight to the point. 'How ill is Mrs Gregson?'

Beryl's entry with the coffee gave the old doctor time to straighten his papers and blow his nose before replying.

'You know, Charlotte,' he said slowly.'That is one of the most difficult questions a doctor has to answer. The fact that you aren't actually a relative. . . .

'I did suggest ringing Derek in America, but she wouldn't hear of it. All I can tell you is that I would be much happier if she would just go into hospital and have some tests done. That would either put her mind at rest, or. . . .'

'Or confirm your suspicions,' Charlotte filled in the missing words. 'I can't promise anything, but I'll see what I can do. I can stay a couple of weeks, at least, so I'll have time to work on her.'

After being cooped up on the train, Charlotte walked to Margaret Gregson's house. Inevitably her thoughts dwelt on the things Doctor Wade had told her – or rather on the things he had not told her.

Was Margaret Gregson really ill? Why wouldn't she do as the old doctor asked? If only Derek wasn't so far away. His mother would have to listen to him.

Suddenly she wished she wasn't the one who had to try and persuade the elderly lady to go into hospital. She found herself lingering, admiring the view. The sea was almost calm, only the faintest ripples of white breaking its surface. Deceptively calm, thought Charlotte, remembering how threatening and angry the waves could be.

There was no point putting the meeting off any longer. She turned away from the sea and was soon walking up the drive.

'Charlotte! What a lovely surprise! Come in – this is nice.'

Charlotte followed the older lady into the small morning-room.

'I use this room all the time now,' Mrs Gregson explained, slightly apologetic. 'Saves work and I always did prefer it.'

The day was quite warm, but a small fire burned in the hearth. As Margaret held out her hands to the warmth, Charlotte noticed the blue veins showing through the almost transparent skin.

Margaret Gregson was small and slight, but she had always been full of vitality. Always busy, polishing and cleaning, working in the garden or the large conservatory. Now, through the french windows, Charlotte could see the neglected plants, even the vine that had been Margaret's pride and joy was a mass of bare strands.

'Well, are you going to tell me why you're here?'

'Oh, I just had a few days' holiday. . . .' Charlotte began.

'Did Doctor Wade ring you?' the other woman interrupted.

Charlotte looked at her. Margaret Gregson was ill, but her mind was as alert as ever. It was no use trying to deceive her.

'Yes!'

'When?'

'On Thursday evening. Margaret, please listen to

me. . . .'

'What did he tell you?' Margaret was not to be put off.

'Only what he has told you. That he would like you to go into hospital for some tests. I think you should do as he says.'

'Nonsense! Oh, I have a few aches and pains, but nothing that won't go away here at home. And if you are thinking of ringing Derek – *don't*.

'He's doing very well in New York. He doesn't say much in his letters but his father's cousin writes to me sometimes, and tells me things he doesn't. In a couple of years or less, he'll be running his own subsidiary company. Then he'll have time to come over here. I can wait until then.'

Charlotte tried to protest, but Margaret waved her into silence.

'Now don't you start worrying about me. I have my home help twice a week and a good neighbour.'

She paused and took a deep breath.

'Don't think I'm not grateful to you for caring. Not many people do now. Everything changed during those seven years we were in America. There's only Annie Willis left from all the neighbours I once had.

'Most of the houses are flats now, and people just haven't time for each other. But Annie's good to me; she does bits of shopping and all that, so I manage fine.'

Margaret leaned over, laying a gentle hand on Charlotte's arm.

'It is nice to see you, love, and I'm sorry if I sound, well, old and obstinate.'

She sighed and tried to explain.

'This is my home, where all my memories are. I want to stay.'

'Oh, Margaret! How do you think Derek will feel when he gets to know? And he'll have to know. *Please*, do as the doctor asks. It will only be for a day or two and if you go now, I'll be able to visit you.'

'I know you mean well, but this is something I have to decide myself. We'll say no more about it just now,' Margaret told her firmly.

'You know your way around,' she continued with a smile. 'Why not go into the kitchen and make us an omelette each. Then you can tell me all your news.'

Sitting alone, Margaret's bravado faded away. The thought of the hospital was never far away. She didn't need the increasing discomfort she was feeling to tell her that Dr Wade was no scaremonger.

If he thought she should go into hospital, then she should.

Margaret closed her eyes, remembering.

She was seven years old, and when her father told her her mother had to go into hospital, he had worded it so that she accepted it without fear.

Margaret had visited the private room several times, reassured by her mother's smile and gentle words. Too young to see the signs of progressive illness, she chatted happily to the sick woman.

One day her aunt took her to the hospital, and, as her father was expected any time, left her with her mother. Tired, Margaret crept into a deep armchair which had been turned to face the window, and fell asleep.

It was the sound of voices that disturbed her. She remembered the brief glimpse of a still, white-shrouded form on the bed, her father's tears. She was still screaming when he carried her out.

Margaret was still afraid of hospitals. Even visiting for a short period made her feel panicky and ill. The thought of going in to stay was unendurable.

She knew she was using Derek's absence as an excuse. The truth was she felt she couldn't explain how she felt. There was no-one who would understand.

With an effort she dragged her mind back to the present.

She had once hoped Charlotte Saunders would become her daughter-in-law. After his father's sudden death in America, Derek had wanted her to stay there, but Margaret had ached to come home to England.

Charlotte had been living at home then, a lovely eighteen-year-old, unable to hide her feelings for the tall, handsome boy her childhood playmate had become.

But just as his mother had yearned for England, so Derek Gregson yearned for America.

They had been back in England a year when her husband's cousin, Raymond Ashton, wrote offering him a post in his newly-formed car telephone service. Margaret had encouraged him to accept.

Only she knew what it cost her. It was goodbye, not only to her son, but to her hopes for Charlotte and the next generation.

Hearing the girl she loved moving about the kitchen gave her a curious sense of sadness.

Sitting quietly by the fire, she found herself thinking wistfully of what might have been.

Three

It was a large kitchen, inconvenient by modern standards, but Charlotte soon found the things she needed. As she worked her thoughts were with her friend. Doctor Wade had not exaggerated, but what could she do? Margaret Gregson was adamant about not going into hospital.

Charlotte set a small table by the window. She found some pretty china and gave the cutlery a rub. Finally she slipped into the garden and cut one or two roses from the neglected bushes.

'Charlotte, how nice! I've got so used to a tray, I hadn't realised how much I miss sitting at a table.'

Margaret leaned over and smelt the deep perfume of the roses; gently, she ran a finger over the soft velvet of the petals. Charlotte thought again of the flowers in the hotel garden; beautiful, living things, with a language all their own.

After they had eaten she carried coffee into the morning room and they sat round the fire again.

'Now then, I want to hear all about London. The new shows – you must have seen some; and boyfriends – I'm sure there is someone?'

Charlotte's heightened colour answered the question.

'But we hardly know each other really,' she added when she had finished telling Margaret about Bill.

Changing the subject she told her about the plays she had seen, and her work at the health centre. By the time she rose to leave, Margaret Gregson was looking much, much better.

Charlotte walked home through the shopping arcade and bought food for the next few days, adding a few delicacies for Mrs Gregson.

At home she put the food away and unpacked. As she did so the question of whether to ring Derek Gregson or not teased her mind.

Would he think she was clutching at any excuse to get in touch with him? Memories of the year he spent in England surfaced. They had revisited old haunts and found new ones. They had danced, played tennis, laughed and teased. He had held her in his arms, his kisses warm, tender.

Charlotte had been so sure he returned her feelings. In the end he had gone without a backward glance. Oh, he had murmured something about seeing each other again, about her joining him in America. But gradually his letters had dwindled, and lately the only news she had had of him was through his mother.

Margaret had been insistent that he shouldn't be told. But if anything happened, what would Derek think if he knew Charlotte could have warned him – and hadn't?

Suddenly Charlotte felt utterly alone. Both her parents had been only children and she had no near relatives. If only her mother was still with her to make her laugh, to advise and conjure up pan muffins for tea.

Tears pricked her eyes, but she blinked them away. She would have a shower and then ring America. Derek had the right to know.

Meanwhile, Bill Menzies smiled as he drove home. He enjoyed his work; he was not ambitious but he loved the earth in all its changing moods.

He thrilled over a patch of bare land, a neglected garden or run-down park, and enjoyed planning what he could make of them. He cared passionately about conservation.

Now he had the satisfaction of knowing his first big commission had come his way. True, he had had to convince his client that a lovely garden didn't mean filling every corner with the expensive and the garish, but Bill knew he could turn the land into a lovely setting for the gracious house he had just left.

When he caught sight of a display of spring flowers, he stopped, remembering Charlotte's pleasure in the gardens the night before. He had thought about her so much, wishing he had told her a little more about how he felt.

He had hoped he might manage a trip to Yorkshire, but with his new commitment it was out of the question.

Impulsively he walked into the shop. The young assistant smiled when he told her what he wanted, then handed him a card.

Bill hesitated, hardly knowing what to say. Then, with a smile he began to write. . . .

Charlotte had just come downstairs when there was a knock on the door. Wondering which of her friends had heard she was home, she answered it.

'Miss Saunders? Interflora!'

Charlotte gasped in surprise as the young man handed her a huge sheaf of flowers. Before she could thank him, he was driving away.

The flowers were beautiful. Daffodils, narcissi, tulips. All the spring flowers she knew and some she didn't.

She opened the small envelope and drew out a card. *A breath of spring – Bill.*

Charlotte removed the wrapping, drinking in the scent. So Bill, too, had remembered the walk in the hotel grounds. A warm glow filled the cold places in her heart. Knowing that Bill cared enough to send the flowers made all the difference. She no longer felt so alone.

Her heart felt lighter as she filled vases. The house was alive once more. Someone cared; someone had thought about her.

Confidently she picked up the telephone and began to dial.

At first Charlotte thought she had the wrong number. Then the girl at the other end spoke again.

'Yes, this is Derek Gregson's apartment.'

'I wanted to speak to him. It's rather important.'

'I'm sorry, but he's away right now. He should be home tomorrow or the day after at the latest. Can I do anything to help?'

'Will you tell him that his mother isn't too well? Ask him if he will ring Charlotte Saunders back as soon as he can?'

Her hands trembled as she replaced the receiver. Who was the girl who sounded so at home in Derek's flat, and why did she, Charlotte, feel so let down, so resentful?

Reaching out, she touched Bill's flowers. How could she reconcile the sudden surge of feeling for Derek, when she thought she was just beginning to care for Bill? Suddenly it was all too much.

She felt the need for air.

Shrugging into an old anorak, she realised the sun had gone in and pulled on a woolly hat as well.

A strong wind was blowing as she walked along the cliffs and she put her hands in her pocket. She smiled as her fingers came in contact with her old woolly gloves.

Charlotte thought of all the times she had run along this path beside Derek. She remembered their laughter, and she remembered those other times when he had brought her close to tears. It was here she had climbed down for the red ball. How terrified she had been. And then he had come to her, helped her.

She walked a little further, then turned back. The wind was getting stronger and she thought about her cosy fireside.

She almost didn't see the blotch of red, bright against the dark brown of the ribbed sand. Charlotte stared, something familiar about the huddled figure stirring her senses.

It was the girl from the bus, the one who had nearly got off at the wrong stop, sitting crouched, hugging her knees, staring out to sea. Surely she knew what danger she was in?

Charlotte cupped her hands round her mouth and

shouted again and again. The wind tossed her words away, losing them in the sound of threatening, crashing waves.

In rising panic she picked up stones, clods of earth, anything, and threw them at the girl. Once she turned, saw Charlotte and turned away again.

She means to drown, thought Charlotte, still not believing. She is sitting there waiting for the tide to come in. And she won't have long to wait.

Charlotte felt terror rising in her as she knew what she had to do. She had to go down the cliff and get the girl. But this time she was alone, there was no Derek to help her now.

Charlotte froze. She felt like a child again – a child forcing herself to face terror. There was a ball, a huge red ball on the beach, and she had to get it.

With a shudder, Charlotte came back to reality. It wasn't a ball! It was a human being. A girl – the girl in the red jacket she had seen on the bus. Didn't she realise the danger? Or didn't she care –

Charlotte took her first hesitant steps to the path. If only she wasn't so afraid – if only her legs would move faster.

Then, as she edged herself down the fear was gone. There was only a sense of urgency; a desperate need to reach the girl before the crashing waves.

She didn't feel the loose shale slithering beneath her feet, grazing her knees as she slipped and grasped at anything to stop herself falling. She didn't feel the buffeting of the wind. All she could think of was the girl. She didn't even dare to look down to see what was happening. A few seconds could make all the difference, and she had already wasted time at the top of the cliff.

'Please,' she whispered. 'Let me be in time.'

Then there was sand beneath her feet. Charlotte ran to where the girl was sitting, her knees hunched, oblivious to what was going on. Only when Charlotte grabbed her shoulder did she turn.

'Come on! You're going to drown.'

'Go away! Leave me alone! I don't want you!'

The girl was struggling, pushing Charlotte away with a strength the older girl wouldn't have thought possible.

'Come on – or you'll die!'

'I know – I deserve to die! I haven't the right to live.'

The words floated out to sea on a wave of anguish. Charlotte had never heard so much pain before, and for a second she stopped pulling. The girl sank back onto the sand.

Charlotte looked down at her and the girl's green eyes reflected the colour of the sea, dark and grey, filled with unfathomable agony.

A wave, bigger than the others, swept up on the beach, covering her hunched knees before it retreated. The cold stung life into the girl, and suddenly she was afraid. Charlotte, no stranger to fear, recognised it and tugged at the girl's hand. This time she allowed herself to be pulled away from the waves.

'Come on! We must go to the next bay,' Charlotte urged frantically.

'No – I can't! The water – '

'There's a better path! Don't waste time arguing – just come.'

Where Charlotte got the strength from to get them round the rocky promontory, she never knew. Perhaps, she thought fancifully, as the waves curled greedily round her legs, Derek is helping me.

Then they were in the next bay, and briefly, very briefly, Charlotte stopped. The girl was gasping great gulps of air, her cold hands clinging to Charlotte.

Then Charlotte was searching for the overgrown path, pushing the frightened girl in front of her.

'Up here. You go first and I'll help.'

Once away from the reach of the hungry waves, the girl tried to help herself. She grabbed at juts of rock, at stunted bushes that loosened under the strain. Charlotte had to dig her feet into the damp, slippery surface to stop them sliding back.

But, bit by bit, they made their way upwards. At last they fell breathless on to the flat, stony surface of the path.

Once she had got her breath back Charlotte sat up. The girl was still stretched out, breathing in short, aching gulps of air. She leaned over and touched her red jacket.

'Come on,' she urged. 'We must move. You're soaked.'

But the girl was sinking back into apathy. Her eyes were empty, as though the brief exertion had been too much for her.

'You go,' she whispered. 'I'll be all right.'

'No, you won't. Not unless you get out of those wet things. Come on now – I'm not moving without you.'

By the time they reached Charlotte's house she was almost dragging the girl, and feeling just about at the end of her tether. Once inside the stranger stood motionless, shivering violently.

Charlotte crossed over to the sideboard and poured

two small glasses of brandy.

'Here, drink it.' She handed one to the girl. 'I don't care whether you like it or not. Then we'll get you into a hot bath.'

The girl didn't argue. She shuddered as the spirit went down, but said nothing. Then she followed Charlotte up the winding staircase and watched expressionlessly as she ran a bath.

Charlotte put an old, but clean, track suit on the chair.

'This will be warm. I'm going to change now. Come down when you're ready.'

As she stripped off her wet clothes and rubbed herself down, Charlotte found herself reliving those moments on the beach. The girl's voice echoed in her mind. *I don't deserve to live.*

Charlotte knew she had not been dramatising. But the agony behind the words would haunt Charlotte for a long time. What could have brought a young girl – no, a woman – to such a state?

By the time her visitor came down Charlotte was heating soup and cutting thick hunks of bread.

'Hello!' she said brightly. 'Are you feeling better?'

The girl nodded. She certainly looked better. Her hair, still damp clung in tight curls round a pale, but charming, face. But for her eyes, guarded and secret, the events of the last two hours might never have happened.

'Don't you think it's time we introduced ourselves? I'm Charlotte Saunders.'

Charlotte smiled as she held out her hand, hoping the girl would respond, and tell her about herself. Instead she touched the extended hand, but only briefly, then drew away. Then, as if knowing it had to be said, she looked at her rescuer.

'Charlotte, you saved my life. Thank you.'

'I don't want thanks. It was only luck I happened to be there. But I do like to know the names of people I have to stay in my home.'

The girl blushed.

'Holly! Holly – Johnston.'

Charlotte noticed the hesitation, as she had noticed the slim gold wedding ring on Holly's left hand, but she said nothing.

'There, I think that's hot enough. You take that tray. I've lit the gas fire and we'll have it on our knee. All nice and cosy, as my mother would have said.'

Charlotte was silent as they ate, but she was watching her guest. Holly nibbled slowly at first, as though reluctant to put herself deeper into Charlotte's debt. Then, as the hot soup warmed her, she ate hungrily until the tray was empty.

It was not until Holly had begun to relax, to curl her feet into the warmth of the chair and cup the beaker of coffee in her hands, that Charlotte spoke again.

'Would you like to use the phone, Holly? Isn't there someone who will be worried about you?'

Immediately the tension was back. Holly uncurled her feet and sat on the edge of the chair, staring into the mock flames of the fire.

'No!' she said abruptly. 'No-one!'

She looked at Charlotte, her eyes defiant.

'I can't go now, but I'll be out of your way tomorrow. As soon as I can get a bus.'

'A bus to where?'

31

Again Holly hesitated, and when she muttered, 'Bristol', Charlotte didn't know whether to believe her or not. But she did know that the young girl was unhappy and confused.

'Holly, I'm not trying to pry.' Her voice was gentle. 'You don't have to tell me anything you don't want to. But, if you would like to stay here for a few days, well – you're very welcome.'

Charlotte saw Holly crumble, as though it was a long time since anyone had been kind to her. She could tell the younger girl was having to fight to keep back the tears.

'Thank you! I – well, can we talk about it tomorrow?'

'Of course. Now, shall we watch television for a while? It might help us both to relax. We'll leave the dishes until morning.'

Long after Holly had gone to bed, Charlotte sat thinking.

What had she done? Taken an unknown girl into her home. A girl who might have given a false name. A girl who was desperately unhappy and refused to say why.

Had she been wrong? Holly's cry on the beach seemed to echo round the small room and again Charlotte felt the pain behind it.

No, she could not have done anything else. She'd had no choice. She'd had to help the girl, and must go on doing so.

The next morning the sun shone, and in spite of her tiredness, Charlotte woke early. Holly's clothes had dried overnight, so Charlotte carried them into the spare room.

Holly was still asleep. For a few seconds, Charlotte stood looking down at her. She looks so young, so vulnerable, she thought. Into her mind drifted the memory of how she had always wished she had a sister. Holly could have been that sister, and she had to fight the temptation to bend over and smooth the tousled hair.

Holly was quiet as they ate breakfast. Charlotte didn't re-open the question of her staying. That was up to the younger girl. It wasn't until Holly was at the sink, washing dishes, her back to Charlotte, that she spoke of the invitation.

'Charlotte – about what you said last night. Can I stay for a day or two? Just until I sort a few things out?'

Charlotte didn't hesitate.

'Of course you can.'

She was packing one or two things to take to Margaret Gregson, and suddenly realised visiting Margaret would mean leaving Holly alone. Remembering the still figure on the beach, the despairing cry, Charlotte felt Holly should not be alone. Not yet.

'I have to go out this morning, to see a friend, take her a few things. Would you like to come with me? I'm sure Margaret would enjoy seeing a new face. Especially one as pretty as yours.'

Holly flushed, as though unused to compliments, but to Charlotte's surprise, agreed at once.

Before they went out Charlotte dialled Bill Menzies' number to thank him for the flowers. There was no reply, and Charlotte felt vaguely let down. She had expected him to be home on a Sunday morning.

Charlotte carefully avoided the cliff path as they walked to Margaret Gregson's. On the way she told

33

Holly a little about her old friend, but mentioned Derek only casually.

As they walked up the path, the door opened and a pleasant woman, a little older than Margaret greeted them.

'You must be Charlotte,' she smiled. 'Margaret has been telling me you're here for a few days. I'm her neighbour, Annie Willis.'

Her voice was cheerful, but as their eyes met, Charlotte could see her own concern mirrored there. But by now Margaret had appeared and Charlotte was introducing Holly.

'A friend of mine. Called unexpectedly, so I asked her to stay a few days.'

Margaret Gregson smiled at the young girl. If the difference in their ages surprised her, she was too polite to say so. She motioned her young visitor to a chair and as they began to talk Charlotte followed Annie Willis into the kitchen.

'Oh, Annie!' Charlotte felt immediately at home with this kindly neighbour. 'She looks so ill!'

'Yes, she has admitted to a bad night. If only she would listen to Doctor Wade. But we can't talk now – she'll know we're discussing her. You carry the coffee in.'

Charlotte was pleased, if surprised, to find Holly and Margaret talking easily. Annie left, promising to look in later in the day.

'Do you know Baynton well?' Margaret was asking.

Charlotte, remembering how Holly had shied away from her questions, held her breath. But Holly smiled at the older woman.

'Yes, I used to come here for holidays. When I was

34

young.'

'Young? You're only young now,' Margaret smiled back at her.

'I'm nineteen, well, nearly nineteen,' Holly amended.

If her two listeners noticed the sudden clouding of her eyes, they said nothing.

'I – I just fancied seeing Baynton again,' she finished, rather lamely.

When Margaret would have spoken, Charlotte shook her head warningly, but after a pause, Holly went on speaking.

'I had an aunt. Well, a sort of aunt – but she's moved. I looked for her, and she wasn't there.'

There was pathos in the simple statement.

'Perhaps I can help,' Margaret said gently. 'I've lived in Baynton a long time. What was her name?'

Holly looked up, hope lighting her features.

'Rose. Rose West.'

Margaret shook her head.

'Sorry, the name doesn't ring a bell. I'll think about it though. I might remember something.'

Holly rose to move the dirty cups, and Charlotte leaned across the table, speaking quietly, but urgently.

'Margaret, you're not well this morning. Please. . . .'

Margaret shook her head. 'Let it be, Charlotte. I'll be better tomorrow.' Then, pointedly changing the subject, she asked:

'Holly. How well do you know her?'

'Not very well, but she needs friends badly. This Rose West? Did you recognise the name?'

'Vaguely. We couldn't accommodate all the guests at our ruby wedding. I think some stayed with a landlady of that name. Annie Willis might know. She used to work in the Advice Bureau and they had a list of guest houses.'

As Holly came into the room, Margaret lay back, closing her eyes. Holly looked at the white face and turned to Charlotte in alarm. So there is room in her heart to think of others, Charlotte thought.

'Margaret, we're going now.' Her friend sat up.

'Must you? We could all have some lunch.'

'Sorry, I'm expecting a telephone call and I don't want to be out.'

Charlotte regretted her words immediately.

Would Margaret guess that the call she was waiting for was from Derek in New York?

'From that young man you were telling me about, I'll be bound. Bill something or other, wasn't it?' Charlotte breathed again.

'Now don't forget, Holly, any time you feel like a walk, just come round. I won't be going very far.' She made a courageous attempt at a laugh, but Charlotte was not deceived.

As they walked away Holly was the first to speak.

'This Bill? Is he the one who sent you those lovely flowers?'

'Yes, but he's only a friend,' Charlotte said hurriedly.

'Some friend,' Holly teased, and Charlotte had a brief glimpse of the laughing young girl she might have been.

'The call I'm expecting isn't from him. It's from Margaret's son Derek in America. I think he should

36

come home.'

'What's wrong with his mother?'

'I don't know. The doctor wants her to go into hospital, but she won't go.'

Charlotte paused and took a deep breath.

'Holly, this Rose West. . . .'

'Oh, it doesn't matter! I shouldn't have mentioned her. She's probably forgotten all about me, anyway.'

Holly's defences were in position again. However there had been a small break-through, Charlotte mused as she prepared the lunch.

Then her thoughts turned to Derek. Margaret was ill – and needed her son – that was evident, but —

The telephone shrilled through the small house.

'Derek?' Charlotte said eagerly as she picked up the receiver.

'Sorry. I'm afraid it's only me – Bill.'

In spite of her efforts Charlotte couldn't hide her disappointment. She knew her voice lacked enthusiasm.

'Bill! How nice. The flowers were lovely. I rang you earlier to thank you, but there was no answer.'

'No! Well I do go out sometimes. As a matter of fact I was at church.'

Bill didn't add that he was thinking of her as he knelt in the quiet peace of the poorly attended church. He knew his words were curt, but he had so looked forward to hearing her voice again.

'Your friend, Mrs Gregson, how is she? I gather you have been in touch with her son?'

'She's quite ill, Bill. I rang Derek, but he was out. I'm expecting a call any time.'

'In that case I'd better leave the line clear. Take care

of yourself,' he added, a gentleness creeping into his voice in spite of his disappointment.

Not waiting to hear more, he replaced the receiver. He was a quiet, unassuming man and was not surprised that Charlotte was eagerly awaiting a call from America. Derek Gregson sounded everything he, Bill, was not. Exciting, well-travelled and a sales executive. It wasn't surprising that Charlotte preferred him to a dull landscape gardener.

Of Derek's mother's illness he thought very little. It never occurred to him that anyone could be too physically afraid to go into hospital. He only knew that soon, Charlotte and her childhood sweetheart would be together.

Bill felt his hopes and dreams crumble as he reached for his drawing board. There was always work.

Charlotte, too, was aware that a gulf had appeared in her relationship with Bill Menzies. She had so looked forward to telling him how the flowers had come just at the right moment, when she needed cheering up; and about Holly.

When Derek did ring she felt it was an anticlimax.

'Your mother's ill, Derek,' she told him quietly.

'But Celia, the girl you talked to, told me you'd just said mother wasn't well.'

'Derek! I've been round this morning. Margaret looks dreadful. She needs to go into hospital at once, and she won't hear of it! You have to come. She'll listen to you.'

'Sorry, Charlotte, I didn't realise. I won't waste time – I'll be on the first flight I can get.'

'You don't know what a relief that is. But your mother told me not to ring, so come here first and we can sort things out.'

'I'll do that. With a bit of luck I'll make it in ten or twelve hours.' He paused. 'And, Charlotte, thank you.'

Charlotte sat back, the relief she felt easing the tension of the last two days. She just hoped the next few hours would not bring further complications.

Four

Meanwhile, in his New York flat, Derek Gregson was quickly, but competently throwing things into suitcases. He was used to flying off at a minute's notice, but this time it was different. He kept hearing the fear in Charlotte's voice.

He was trying to force the lid down on one of the cases when Celia Hammerton walked in. She looked round in amazement.

''Derek! Oh, don't say you've to go away now.'

'Sorry, Celia. I've been talking to Charlotte Saunders. I have to go home. Mother's ill. She needs me.'

'But that's the girl I spoke to. She just said Mrs Gregson was not well.'

'She's worse now. Celia,' he added gently. 'Charlotte isn't one to panic. If she thinks I'm needed, well, I have to go.

'I rang the airport. They said to go at once and stand by. One seat shouldn't be too difficult to find.'

'You might have to wait ages,' Celia protested. 'Couldn't we just go out tonight? I've been looking forward to it.'

Celia knew Derek was not as deeply attracted to her as she was to him, but she'd had high hopes for tonight. Her dress had cost far more than she could afford and she had spent ages in the beauty salon. Time she could barely spare from her job as a fashion buyer.

Derek took her in his arms.

'Sorry, love, but I have to go. I'll get in touch as soon as possible. You can stay here until your own flat is ready for you to move back into. Just give the keys to the janitor. And Celia, we'll make up for tonight another time.'

Celia sensed his anxiety and knew she would have to let him go. She drew his dark head down and kissed him. For a moment, as his lips were on hers, firm and demanding, she felt him weakening. Then, abruptly he released her.

'I've left my address on the desk.'

Briefly their eyes met, then, picking up his cases, he was gone.

Oh, Charlotte she thought, couldn't you have waited? Just another day —

Holly Johnston had fallen asleep. Charlotte watched the rise and fall of her breathing and heard a low moan as the young girl turned in the chair. Even in sleep. Holly was troubled.

Charlotte, too, was uneasy. The relief she had felt when she knew Derek would soon be home was now confused with the realisation that soon she and Derek would be together again.

Would the years in America have changed him very much? Would he still care? Still want to be with her?

41

Suddenly she felt very vulnerable. Twice she had grieved over her partings with Derek, and twice he had made promises which he hadn't kept.

In London she had worked hard to build up a new life. How many times had she told herself that Derek would have no part in it, determined that she was not going to be hurt again?

And what of Bill? Dear, kind, gentle Bill who cared so desperately about all living things. How could she feel such tenderness towards him, yet have such an up-surge of feeling at the thought of seeing Derek again?

Charlotte leaned over, and touched Bill's flowers. They were fading a little, but still lovely, still fragrant.

Suddenly Charlotte felt Holly's eyes on her. The young girl had come out of her restless sleep and was smiling as she watched the older girl gently touching the blooms.

'They're lasting well,' Holly said softly. 'You're like me. I hate throwing flowers out, especially when they are from someone special.'

'But they're—' Charlotte broke off. How could she explain to Holly feelings she couldn't explain to herself?

Instead she rose briskly to her feet.

'I'll see how that casserole is doing. You can lay the table.'

Holly followed Charlotte into the kitchen.

'When is Derek arriving?'

'Sometime in the early hours of the morning, I imagine. He seemed to think he'd soon get a flight. I'll have an early night and be up when he comes. You sleep on, if you can.'

42

But it was after eight o'clock in the morning when Derek arrived and both girls were up.

As soon as Charlotte opened the door and saw his ravaged face, the hollow tiredness in his eyes, her doubts fled. He was just Derek, needing her assurance, her help.

'Derek! You look worn out! Here, give me your coat. Dump everything else in the hall. I've breakfast all ready to cook.'

'No food, thank you. Just a huge pot of tea.'

As she took his coat, their eyes met. In spite of the apprehension they were both feeling, they smiled fleetingly. Then Charlotte answered the question Derek was afraid to ask.

'Your mother said she was feeling a lot better when I rang last night. I know you want to see her straight away, but you should eat something first.'

'No, I must—' He broke off as Holly came into the room carrying a plate of bacon and scrambled egg.

'A friend of mine,' Charlotte explained. 'Holly Johnston. Now come on, Derek. Sit down.'

He did just that, but ate quickly.

'What are you going to say to your mother? She'll be furious with me for calling you?'

'Don't worry, I'll think of something. I won't get you into trouble this time.'

Remembering all the times Derek had done just that, they both laughed. He stood up.

'You were right, I needed that. Now I must go. I'll ring you.'

There was sudden silence in the room as the telephone shrilled.

Charlotte picked it up. Derek and Holly moved

closer together as they saw her face change.

'It's your mother! Annie Willis found her collapsed on the floor by her bed. She should be in hospital by now.'

Oddly, it was the shock on Holly's face more than Derek's stricken look that jerked Charlotte into action.

'I'll get a coat,' she said quickly. 'Derek, there's a number for a taxi on the pad near the phone. Holly, you'd better come with us. It will be better than waiting here, not knowing.'

Her matter of factness had the desired effect.

Derek, his usual quick reactions dulled by the night of travel and anxiety, began to dial. Holly followed Charlotte upstairs and in seconds, they were ready. But as Charlotte made to go back down, Holly spoke, her voice raw with pain.

'Why do people we love have to die, Charlotte? So many horrible people live, but the old and the young, too small to have done any harm.' Her voice broke.

'Later, love,' Charlotte said gently. 'We must get to the hospital now.'

Somehow she knew it was not Mrs Gregson who was uppermost in Holly's mind – then who?

As they went out to the taxi she looked at Derek and saw the reflection of her own fear. What if they were too late? If he could never tell his mother how much he cared.

At the hospital a young nurse greeted them.

'I'm sorry, but the specialist is still with Mrs Gregson. If you wait here I'll keep you in touch.'

The half-hour wait in the hospital corridor seemed endless.

Charlotte was not aware that Derek had taken her

hand until she felt her ring cutting into her finger. In spite of the discomfort, she left it there; it felt oddly comforting.

Holly was hunched at the end of the bench, her face closed, her hands deep in her pockets.

Charlotte and Derek stood up as an elderly, white coated gentleman came up to them, his face grave, unsmiling.

'You're Mrs Gregson's son? Nurse said you were here.'

Derek nodded. 'Please, how is she?'

'Your mother is in a critical condition. If she had seen me earlier. . . .' He paused and shook his head.

'I understand from the neighbour who came with her that you have just flown back from New York?'

Again Derek could only nod.

'But you didn't go straight home? You went to your –' he hesitated, 'your friend's home.'

Only then did Charlotte realise Derek was still gripping her hand. She could feel his guilt as he released it.

'Doctor—'

'*Mister* Sawyer,' the specialist corrected.

'I went to Miss Saunders to find out how Mother was. Mother had asked her not to send for me.'

Both Derek and Charlotte realised how feeble his words were. How could a stranger understand?

'Otherwise,' Mr Sawyer continued, as though Derek had not spoken, 'your mother may have had attention sooner. We have no idea how long she was lying on the floor. It might have been for hours.'

Derek didn't attempt to justify himself further.

'But what is it, Mr Sawyer? What is wrong with my

mother?'

The specialist shook his head. But his voice was softer when he spoke again. Perhaps he recognised Derek's fear of the answer.

'I'm not in a position to say yet. If we can build up her strength, we'll do some tests. Until then—'

'Can I see her?'

Mr Sawyer hesitated.

'Please,' Derek urged. 'I had no idea she was ill until yesterday. I came as soon as I could get a flight.'

'Very well. After I've checked again. Five minutes. No longer.'

He glanced at Holly, still sitting hunched on the bench.

'You all right?' he asked gently.

Holly looked up and nodded.

'Yes, thank you. But please, please look after Mrs Gregson.'

Derek sank back on the bench as Mr Sawyer moved away. Charlotte looked down at him.

'Derek, you look all in. Are you fit to see your mother?'

He lifted haggard eyes to hers. Lack of sleep, guilt, jet lag, it was all there. But his voice was firm.

'I must, Charlotte. It might be my only chance to . . . .'

Then the nurse was back.

'Mr Gregson, you can go in now.'

Derek was glad there was no-one near him to see his tears as he sat beside his mother. It was not the tubes attached to her body, he had been prepared for those. It was her appearance that shocked him.

Always slightly built, her body scarcely lifted the

bedclothes from the bed. Her face was as white as the sheets. Only her hands on the coverlet moved slightly.

'Oh, Mother,' he whispered brokenly. 'If only I'd known.'

'You two sit down,' Holly Johnston told them when they got back to Charlotte's. 'I'll make some coffee.'

Charlotte and Derek sat at each side of the fireplace, grateful for the warmth. When Holly came in with the tray, she curled up on the rug. Derek moved a little so she could lean back.

She's lovely, Charlotte thought, and she doesn't even know it.

Derek, too, was looking down at the bent head, and his eyes were gentle. He glanced across at Charlotte, and smiled.

For a moment, they shared their affection for this mystery girl and forgot their deeper worries.

But not for long. Derek stood up and put down his empty cup.

'Derek,' Charlotte said hesitantly. 'You need some sleep desperately. I could get a bed ready.'

He shook his head.

'Thanks, but I'd better get home. I must see Annie Willis, and thank her for what she's done. Can I collect my bags later?'

Charlotte nodded and he went on.

'Will you come to the hospital with me this afternoon? I could meet you there at two o'clock. If we don't hear anything before then,' he finished slowly.

Charlotte crossed over and took his hands.

'We won't,' she whispered with more confidence than she felt. 'Get some sleep and things will look

47

better.'

If they had been alone, she might have reached up and kissed him. Instead a gentle pressure of the hands was all she allowed herself. Then he was gone.

As Derek Gregson walked home alone, the feeling of guilt and inadequacy he had felt at the hospital returned.

He had intended going to see Annie Willis, but suddenly he knew he could not cope with any more. He picked up the telephone.

'She's holding her own,' he told the kindly neighbour. 'I'll come and see you after I've been to see her this afternoon. I'm going to bed now.'

Too tired to make up his own bed, he crept into his mother's.

Her presence still lingered and he felt close to her again. Before his thoughts could go back to the hospital, he was asleep.

Derek and Charlotte sat one on each side of the bed. Margaret Gregson didn't move until their time with her was nearly over. Then, briefly, she opened her eyes.

'Derek, is it you? I thought I had dreamed it. Your voice—'

He bent over the bed, kissing the white cheek.

'And Charlotte—'

They had to bend low to hear.

'I told you not to bring him – but the young always think they know best. Perhaps they do.'

Her eyes closed again but her hand groped across the covers and Derek took it between his own. A hint of a smile played momentarily across the still face, then she was asleep again.

As they left the hospital the air was warm with May sunshine.

Derek asked Charlotte to walk with him along the cliffs.

She hesitated, thinking of Holly on her own, but the thought of a few hours with Derek was too tempting.

They walked in silence for a while, but as they left the few houses behind, Derek spoke.

'I didn't know how much I'd missed Baynton until now.'

'And how long will it be before you are missing New York?' asked Charlotte lightly, thinking about the girl who had answered her call to his flat.

'I don't know. I like the life and there are great opportunities in the business world, but – well, if anything had happened to mother before I got here. I'd never have forgiven myself. She must be my first concern. Perhaps I'll stay here.' He shrugged.

He turned to his companion. He was taller now than Charlotte. Neither of them bore much resemblance to the children who had once walked the cliff path together. Only their pleasure in each other's company was the same. Derek slipped an arm round her shoulders.

'And you, Charlotte? How do you like London?'

'It's hard work with not too much money attached.' Charlotte grinned. 'But I enjoy it.'

So they walked on, talking about their different lives, until they reached the bay.

'Remember the red ball?' Derek asked.

Charlotte nodded. She remembered a girl as well. In spite of the warmth of the day, she shivered.

'Hey, surely it wasn't as bad as that,' Derek teased. 'You know I wouldn't have let anything happen to you.'

The urge to confide in someone, to ask advice, washed over her.

'Let's sit down,' she suggested. 'I want to talk to you.'

So Charlotte told him how she had found Holly on the beach. And soon, Derek too, found himself caught up in the mystery.

'But she's only a kid! She can't be in that much trouble.'

'She's eighteen and married, and very unhappy. She's better now than when I found her, but—'

Even to Derek, Charlotte couldn't bring herself to repeat Holly's desperate words – *I'm not fit to live*.

'I have to help her, Derek,' she said instead.

'And you don't know anything about her husband, or her family?'

'Not a thing. If I ask her she shuts up like a clam. I'm afraid of driving her away, and then goodness knows what would happen to her.

'I could be wrong about her being married, but I don't think so. I've seen her looking at her ring, touching it.

'The only clue I have is this Rose West.'

'Poor Charlotte. My troubles, and now Holly's. If there is anything I can do, once Mother is a little better – you know I will.

'Come on now, we'd better get back. Shall I walk you home?'

Charlotte shook her head.

'But you will let me know if there's any news?'

'Of course I will.' Gently, he touched her cheek. 'Oh, Charlotte, what would I have done without you?'

'Remember the last time I was here? When I brought Mum home after Dad died? Our magic year, I used to call it.'

'Of course I remember.'

How could she ever forget the closeness between the seventeen-year-old girl and the nineteen-year-old boy? Their kisses and their laughter. And the dreams she had woven round them?

She looked up at him and he traced the curve of her mouth with a gentle finger.

'Dear Charlotte,' he whispered. His kiss was sweet and tender.

It was late that evening when Derek rang.

'Mother's just the same,' he told her. 'I've seen Annie Willis and thanked her.'

They chatted casually for a few minutes before Derek rang off, and Charlotte wondered at her feeling of being let down. Derek meant nothing to her now. Her feelings lay elsewhere, didn't they?

She took a few more dead blooms from the flowers Bill Menzies had sent. The others would last another day.

She remembered how he'd sounded on the phone when she'd told him about Derek coming home. It saddened her to think she had hurt him. She must write, but not tonight. She was too weary, too emotionally drained.

Charlotte slept till the early hours, then sat up, listening. The sounds that had disturbed her were coming from Holly's room.

Grabbing a dressing-gown, she went into the small

bedroom. Holly was still asleep, but her arms were thrashing wildly and most of the covers were on the floor.

'No,' she moaned. 'No – it isn't true. Don't let it be true! Roger, help me – make him better.'

'Holly!' Charlotte sat on the bed and put her arms round the shaking girl, but Holly pushed her away.

'It isn't my fault. It isn't!'

But perhaps even in her sleep she knew Charlotte was there, trying to comfort her. Her voice faltered to a stop and she lay still.

The green grey eyes, dark in the shadows of the room, opened.

'I had a dream,' Holly whispered. 'It keeps coming. . . .'

'Tell me about it,' Charlotte said gently.

Holly shook her head.

'It's gone now. I'm sorry I woke you. I'll be all right now.'

'You're frozen, and I'm not too warm either. I'll make us both a hot drink.'

But, when Charlotte returned, Holly's defences were back in place. She had straightened the bed and slipped an old cardigan of Charlotte's round her shoulders.

'Go back to bed, Charlotte. It was just a silly dream.' But her voice trembled, and her hands holding the beaker, shook.

Charlotte carried her own drink back to her room and lay thinking. Roger? Who was he? Holly's father – or perhaps her husband?

Then her thoughts turned to Rose West. *I looked for her and she wasn't there*, Holly had said.

If Rose West could help Holly, then she should try to find her.

Margaret had suggested asking Annie Willis. But she must not raise Holly's hopes, just in case — .

Five

'Why are you so good to me?' Holly asked the next morning.

It was a question Charlotte had asked herself, one to which she found no answer. 'Oh, just because. . . .' she replied lightly.

'I can't go on sponging on you, though,' Holly went on. 'I thought I'd write to my landlady. I can trust her not to—' she broke off, flushing.

'Not to tell anyone,' Charlotte finished for her, silently.

'There will be a Social Security cheque for me and she'll send it on. I need a few more clothes or these will be washed away! Then I'll try and get a job. For the summer, anyway.'

'Holly, just take things as they come. You're welcome here as long as you care to stay.' Charlotte smiled, reassuringly.

'I have some business to attend to. I might be away most of the day. You'll be all right on your own, won't you?'

She looked at the heavy-eyed girl sitting opposite

her.

'You won't do anything silly?'

Holly shook her head.

'You don't have to worry. I won't do anything like that again.' A pause. 'Don't you want to see Derek? He'll be coming round for his bags.'

Charlotte had already decided she wouldn't mind missing Derek. He had hurt her twice; she would not risk it a third time.

'No, I'll see him later. You'll be in. Now – will you slip round to the shops for me while I get changed?'

As soon as Holly had gone, Charlotte rang Annie Willis.

'Rose West. That was the name Margaret mentioned, wasn't it?

'I've been thinking about it and I seem to remember she ran a boarding-house called Elmview. Nothing classy, but good food and spotlessly clean. We sent her quite a few people from the Advice Centre.

'She left about four years ago to go and stay with her brother in Scarborough. His wife wasn't well. She could have stayed in Scarborough – but I'm not sure. I'll keep my ears open, though, and try to find out.'

'Thanks, Annie! I'll let you know how I get on.'

Charlotte's first visit was to Elmview. She looked in distaste at the peeling paint, the flaking stuccowork, and at the spiky red hair of the shabby youth who answered the door.

'Rose West! Had a lass asking t'other day. What's she done? Robbed a bank or something?'

Laughing at his own humour, he began to close the door. Charlotte put her foot in it.

'She must have left a forwarding address. Aren't

there any older tenants here?'

The youth glowered. 'There's old Jeff. I'll get him.'

Old Jeff shuffled to the door in his carpet slippers, his watery eyes peering at Charlotte as he spoke.

'Aye, lassie, I remember Rose. Had a room at 'er place for years. A right grand 'un she were. Not like this lot. Should have got out a long time since.

'Went to 'er brother's, she did. Bernard Cosgrove 'is name was. I can remember it 'cause I 'ad a teacher at school called that. Not that he taught me much.' The old man gave a throaty chuckle.

'And is Rose still with her brother?' Charlotte tried to keep him to the point.

'No, didn't work out. I knowed from the start it wouldn't. Not with a missus like he 'ad. Rose came a time or two to see me, and I could tell. Don't know where she went then. Fancied running a little cafe. Fine cook she were.'

'Do you remember a little girl called Holly?'

'Holly?' The old man's grubby fingers grated against the whiskery growth as he rubbed his chin.

'Ay now – a bonnie little lass. Rose were right fond of 'er. Left 'er on 'er own too much 'er dad did. That busy with 'is fossil hunting or some'at. Rose looked after 'er, though. Could have been 'er own they were that close. Don't know what 'appened to 'er either, though.

'Would you like a cup o' tea, Missus? Can soon put the kettle on.'

Charlotte hated herself for the disappointment her refusal obviously caused, but she really hadn't time and she had learned all she could.

Soon she was on the bus heading for Scarborough,

where she went to the post office and studied the telephone directory.

'Bernard Cosgrove?' she asked.

There was a slight hesitation before a rather grating voice answered.

'No, I'm Mrs Cosgrove.'

'I do hope you can help. I'm trying to get in touch with his sister, Rose West—'

'Well, I can't.' All pretence of politeness was gone. 'Came to live here, but we weren't good enough for her. Dear me, no! Now Bernard's gone as well and I don't know where either of them are. Don't care much either.'

Charlotte heard the receiver slammed back into place. A thoroughly unpleasant woman, she thought. No wonder kindly Rose West had left.

Charlotte wasn't very hopeful as she leafed through the yellow pages. There was no mention of West at all. It was only as she was replacing the heavy volume that a thought occurred to her. Quickly she looked back – *Elmview Tea Room* – was it possible?

Charlotte scribbled the address down, and conscious that time was passing, took a taxi to the address. Elmview Tea Room was not very large, but attractively laid out.

For a few minutes she just stood. Inside was one pretty young waitress, and a slightly older person, but no-one who could possibly be Rose West. Was she to be unlucky again?

She felt her hopes sink, but having come so far, she might as well make some enquiries. There was a soft tinkle of the bell as she pushed open the door.

Inside the cafe was larger than it looked. The

atmosphere was pleasant, the tables colourful with pastel tablecloths and small flower arrangements.

Charlotte stood hesitantly, looking round. There were two young girls carrying trays, and an older woman, slim, with dark hair and large spectacles.

The older woman came up to her, smiling.

'Good afternoon! A table for one?'

Charlotte shook her head.

'Actually, I'm looking for someone. But I'm not sure. Her name is Rose West.'

A cautious look crossed the woman's expressive face.

'Rose West? You're a friend of hers?'

'No – we've never met. But. . . .'

'Then what made you think you might find her here?'

'Because I knew she was in Scarborough, and the name of the cafe. She used to run a boarding-house called Elmview in Baynton.'

At that point a small crowd of laughing holiday-makers crowded in. The woman touched Charlotte's arm, leading her to a small table tucked away almost out of sight.

'Look, I'm Marion Formby. You're right. Rose does own this cafe, but I'm not sure that she'll want to see you. Could I help?'

'No, it's just that I've met a friend of hers, and I wanted to talk.'

Whether Marion Formby would have relented, Charlotte wasn't to find out. They were interrupted by a gaunt, grey-haired woman who leant heavily on a thick walking-stick.

'What is it, Marion? Anything I can help with?'

'Oh, Rose! I wasn't going to trouble you, but this young lady wanted to see you. I wasn't sure. . . .' she finished hesitantly.

Charlotte's heart sank as she looked disbelievingly at the newcomer. Was this woman Rose West? She couldn't be!

'I'm Rose West.' She was holding out a hand. 'I don't think we've met. I would have remembered.'

'No. I'm Charlotte Saunders.' Her mind was racing. Surely there was no help here for a young, unhappy girl.

Marion's quiet voice broke the silence.

'You mentioned a friend of Mrs West's?'

'Yes, a young girl. Holly Johnston.'

Rose shook her head, but not before Charlotte had seen the flicker of memory in her eyes.

'I once knew a Holly Webster. A bonny child.'

Charlotte nodded.

'She married. I didn't know her maiden name. But I shouldn't be here. I don't think I should trouble you.'

'You already have.' A smile lit up her whole face, robbing the words of any sting. 'I have a flat upstairs. We'd better talk there.

'Sally,' she turned to one of the waitresses. 'Bring a tray of tea and scones up to my sitting-room when you have time, my dear.'

Rose West led the way. Charlotte hung back, watching the slow, clumsy climb up the shallow stairs.

What had Holly said about Rose. *She was so soft and cuddly*.

Rose's sitting room was furnished in bright, cheerful colours. The chairs and the settee covered in flowered linen, the carpet and curtains picking up the colours.

Rose sank exhausted on to a high-seated chair, but, after a few seconds smiled at Charlotte.

'Come on now, sit down and tell me about Holly.'

Before Charlotte could answer, Sally appeared with a tray. She put it in front of her employer and asked if she should pour.

'Of course not, Sally. Don't *you* start fussing.' There was a trace of impatience in her voice.

Charlotte forced herself to stay still as she watched Rose rest the lip of the jug on the cups as she poured the milk; watched her fingers run over the rim of the cup before she bent low to pour the tea.

Charlotte placed her own cup on a small table and took one of the scones.

'Now, tell me about you and Holly. I suspect this isn't just a social visit. Does Holly know you're here?'

'No! Look, Mrs West. I don't think I should trouble you—'

'As I said before, you already have. So hadn't you better say why you came?'

Charlotte saw she had gone too far to draw back.

'I met Holly on the beach last Saturday. We talked together and both got soaked. So I took Holly home with me to dry out.

'She was lost and unhappy. Her marriage had broken up and she had come to Baynton to find you, only you weren't there.

'She won't talk about her past, but I think she needs to. All her unhappiness seems to be locked inside her. She had a nightmare and talked about someone called Roger.'

Rose West had sat through Charlotte's words without showing any emotion.

'Has she said anything about her father?' she asked finally.

Charlotte shook her head.

'No, I wondered if Roger was. . . .'

'No, I knew her father well, and her mother before she died. Her father was Sam Webster.'

Rose was staring into space now, lost in thought.

'He was a decent bloke. I liked him, but he thought more about his job, or rather, hobby, than he did about Holly. He would leave her with me most of the summer holidays. Not that I minded, we had lovely times together.

'But when Holly started going on holidays with the school, we lost touch.

'So she got married! She must have been little more than a child. Whatever was Sam thinking of to allow it?'

'Mrs West. I'm sorry if I've. . . .'

'You came to ask me to help Holly, didn't you?'

'Yes, but. . . .'

'My dear young woman.' Rose's eyes twinkled and Charlotte caught a glimpse of the person Holly had described. 'I know I'm stiff, well that's an understatement, and I don't see too well. But I wouldn't let that stop me going to Holly if I thought that was the best thing for her.'

When she hesitated Charlotte spoke without thinking.

'Surely there's something the doctors can do?'

'They're doing what they can.' There was no trace of self-pity in Rose's voice.

'But what about Holly? You say she is staying with

you in Baynton? For how long?'

'I don't know.'

'I'll have her father's address somewhere.'

'No, if Holly wanted him, she could write herself. We can't approach him without asking her. That would make her feel there was no-one she could trust.'

'Leave it with me, I need time to think,' Rose said quietly.

'But don't tell Holly where I am. I'll get in touch if I feel it is the right thing to do.

'Now, Charlotte, if I may call you that – let's have another cup of tea and you can tell me a bit about yourself.'

When her visitor left, Rose stood by the window, watching the blurred form move away. Then she crossed over to the sideboard and took out some photograph albums.

Her sight was further marred by tears as she peered at the familiar faces. Happy groups on the seashore; Holly in the garden of Elmview; Holly, wet from the sea scrambling on the rocks.

In some of them, a tall grey-haired man appeared. Rose looked at him and remembered his young wife. If she had lived things would have been so different. After her death, Sam retreated further into himself and spent even less time with his daughter.

Even so, Rose had liked him; if she were honest, perhaps more than liked him, and had never doubted his love for his little girl.

One day sprang alive in Rose's memory. Nine-year-old Holly had flung her arms round Rose's neck and hugged her.

'Oh, Auntie Rose. I wish you were my mummy.'

'So do I, love, but we can pretend when you come to stay. An auntie is the next best thing to a mummy, and I love you as much as if you were my little girl.'

'That's lovely then. Mummies look after girls and when mummies get old girls look after them. I'll always look after you, Auntie Rose.'

If Holly saw her like this – Rose shivered. It would just be another worry for someone with enough problems of her own.

No, it would be far better if she knew nothing. At least until after Rose's next eye operation. The specialist had tried to be kind, but she had demanded the truth.

'I think you should carry on until you have nothing to lose either way,' he had told her gently. 'Then we will see what we can do.'

That had been eight months ago, and Rose knew she could not carry on much longer. And if the worst happened and the operation failed.

A minute blood clot had rendered one eye useless, and in spite of a successful cataract operation a membrane was now clouding the other.

Well, if things didn't work out, Holly would never know. At eighteen she had her whole life in front of her. She would probably go back to her husband, sort her life out. She was too young to tie herself to an ailing woman.

Rose put her albums on the table, washed her face and made her slow, painful way downstairs. There was always something she could do to help.

Her heart, though, was heavy. It grieved her that Holly needed her help and she was unable to give it.

Charlotte was very depressed as she made her way home.

She had hoped for so much if she was successful in finding Rose West. Now she knew that Rose would not be able to help Holly. Should she have tried harder? Told her how deeply unhappy Holly really was? No, Rose had enough to cope with.

Her spirits lightened though when she arrived home. Holly had tidied up and had the kettle boiling.

'Mind if I go out for a while? I didn't like leaving the house empty, in case there was a telephone call or anything.'

'Of course not! You go out and get some air.'

When Holly left, Charlotte lay back in her chair feeling as though everything in her life was going wrong. She had just closed her eyes when the telephone rang.

'Bill! What a lovely surprise! I was going to write, but this is nicer.'

'Actually.' The word, spoken in his deep voice, with his slightly southern accent, was a little hesitant. 'Actually, I rang to ask you to be sure to let me know when you'll be home. I'll meet the train.'

'I've still more than a week of my leave left. I'm not sure.'

'I know, but I'm missing you, Charlotte. I hoped you might come back a day or two earlier. We could spend the time together.'

'Bill, I'm sorry, but I just don't know. I might have to stay here longer. I was thinking of applying for extended leave without pay.'

Charlotte spoke slowly, plans forming in her mind. 'It's an easy time at the Health Centre, they'll soon be having students for training. They might be able to sub-let my flat—'

'But, Charlotte, why? You went to look after your friend, but she has her son with her now.'

'There's Holly. I told you about her in my letter.'

'Love, you can't spend your time looking after any waif and stray. Besides, you said she was married.

'Charlotte, my dearest Charlotte—' His voice dropped and she could hear the pleading, the courage he was making himself find to overcome his usual reticence. 'Come back, love. We need to talk. Don't you ever think about me – us?'

'Of course I do, but somehow, being back in Baynton has done something to me. Give me a little more time, please! I'll write to you.'

'Are you sure it's Baynton that's the attraction? Perhaps it's Derek Gregson. If so, I'm sorry I troubled you. I'd better go.'

'Bill, it isn't Derek—'

But the line was dead.

Charlotte sat back in her chair. Until a few moments ago she hadn't thought of extending her stay. Now the thought of another two months or so in her old home filled her with a sense of peace, of belonging.

Oh, she loved London. And she loved her job, so much so that she had not come home during the past two years. But now —

At the other end of the line, Bill Menzies was also lost in thought. Not an assertive man, he rarely pushed himself forward. Now, however, a quiet determination not to lose Charlotte without a fight filled his heart.

They'd spoken twice on the telephone and both calls

had ended in misunderstandings. Perhaps if he could talk to her.

He pulled his diary towards him. If he worked all weekend and put in some extra hours on Monday, he would be far enough ahead to set off for Yorkshire on Tuesday.

Derek walked into the small ward. His eyes lit up with pleasure when he saw his mother in a chair beside the bed.

'Mother, you're up!'

'Not really, dear. The doctor thought changing my position might help. You've talked to the specialist?'

Derek took his mother's thin hand in his own strong brown one.

'There's nothing wrong with you that can't be put right. A spot of anaemia and a trace of diabetes. You'll have to stay here until they get the various doses of medicine sorted out, then we'll have you home again.'

Margaret nodded. 'They're very good to me.'

She squeezed his fingers. 'I can't talk much, but I can listen. Tell me about your life in New York.'

So Derek told her about his work and his hopes. He described his modern flat with the picture windows looking over the city.

'And this girl you've mentioned in your letters? Celia something or other?'

'Celia?'

Margaret noticed the affection in his voice when he said her name.

'What can I say? Celia is a New York girl. Bright, pretty, ambitious. She's a buyer for one of the top stores and always in a whirl. Any time now she will be jetting off to Europe to choose a range of clothes from the big fashion houses.'

'She's written?'

Derek laughed.

'No, Mother. The Celias of this world don't write letters. They just pick up the nearest telephone. She rang last night.'

He looked towards the door.

'Here comes the nurse to see you into bed. I'd better go. I'm still under instructions not to stay long.'

Margaret smiled at the young nurse as she helped her gently back into bed. Why had she been so afraid to come into hospital? How silly she must have seemed. Now she was no longer afraid of her memories; the horror of that dreadful day when her mother had died, had gone. Perhaps one day she would talk about it to Derek and Charlotte.

But it wasn't Derek and Charlotte, she thought as she drifted off to sleep. It was Derek and Celia. Charlotte Saunders had her Bill.

Six

It was Monday morning when Holly received an answer to her letter to Bristol. She took out her social security cheque and looked at it for a few seconds without speaking.

'Oh, Charlotte!' she burst out. 'I hate living on hand-outs. It does something to you, something demoralising. I'm going to get some clothes and look for a job. Clothes are expensive, though. Is there a Save the Children shop or an Oxfam anywhere? I've had things from them before and they were fine.'

'I don't think there is anything like that round here. But I have seen one, and recently. Now where was it? Oh, I remember! It was on the same road as Rose West's cafe.'

Her voice faltered as she realised what she had said. Holly's cheque fluttered unnoticed to the floor and she stared at Charlotte.

'You've seen Auntie Rose? You've actually talked to her and not told me? You knew how much I wanted her!' Her voice rose shrilly. 'That was why I came here, to find her and you've kept me away from her. . . .'

'Holly, it isn't like that! Mrs West didn't want me to tell you.'

'I don't believe you. Auntie Rose would always want me, I know that. I thought you were my friend, I trusted you – I nearly told you about. . . .' She broke off, gasping for breath, her eyes reflecting her disbelief.

As Charlotte made to take her hands, she backed away.

'Holly! Mrs West didn't want me to tell you where she is because she isn't well. She. . . .'

'I don't believe you,' Holly repeated. 'I think you just want to keep me here with you. Don't you understand she was like a mother to me? I need her! Just write her address down and I'll pack my things. That won't take long!'

There was an air of bleakness about the young girl as she returned wearing her shabby red jacket. Charlotte knew all the trust she had built up between them had been shattered. Holly felt on her own again – let down. How would she fare when she met Rose West?

Regretfully Charlotte handed Holly the piece of paper with Rose's address on. For a moment the eyes of the two girls met, then Holly turned and walked away.

As Charlotte tidied the breakfast dishes, she realised how much she had enjoyed Holly Johnston's company. Had that something to do with her deciding to stay longer in Baynton?

Anyway, it was too late to change her mind now. Her extended leave was already arranged, and when Beryl Burton, the doctor's receptionist left the following week to have her baby, Charlotte had agreed to stand in for her.

Suddenly Charlotte felt the need to talk, and her thoughts went to Derek Gregson. They had met at the hospital, but he had not suggested them spending time together. He had looked tired. Spending too much time on that paperwork from New York, his mother had said. Well, she would drag him away from it.

Charlotte changed and applied a touch of make-up. Then, satisfied that she looked reasonably good, she walked quickly round to the Gregsons' house.

She stared at the apparition that opened the door. It was Derek, wrapped in one of his mother's overalls, his hair speckled with blue paint. Wiping his hands on an old rag that smelt strongly of turps, he looked at her ruefully as she followed him inside.

'I thought you were busy with paperwork,' Charlotte grinned.

He led her into the kitchen, and she looked round speechlessly at the patchy, half painted walls and the streaky ceiling.

'That's what I wanted Mum to think. I thought it would be a surprise for her. It needed doing.'

Charlotte stifled a giggle.

'It will be a surprise all right! But why didn't you get someone in?'

'I thought she would like to know I had done it myself. I wanted her to know, well, that I was thinking about her.'

Charlotte began to laugh.

'Oh, Derek, you haven't changed after all. Still getting into scrapes. If only you could see yourself!'

Their eyes met and suddenly the years rolled away.

She was in his arms, his lips warm on hers. She put her arms round him, and returned his kisses. She felt at last she was where she belonged.

'Oh, my dear, dear Charlotte, why didn't I take you back with me to America? Why did I let you slip out of my grasp?'

Charlotte drew away and touched his face with a gentle hand.

'Because I was too young, and you were too ambitious, and too poor.'

'We'd have managed somehow. Is it too late, darling? Have we grown too far apart?'

Charlotte dropped her head on his shoulder and was quiet for a while. She had dreamed of this so often. But it had always taken place in romantic places, not a half-painted kitchen – with Derek half painted as well.

Why didn't she just tell Derek that she loved him? That nothing else mattered? Was it because, deep down, she still remembered how easily, and how often he had hurt her in the past?

The moment passed, and she drew away.

'I know it will be too late to do much to your poor mother's kitchen if we don't get a move on. Find me something to wear and I'll tackle the walls while you give the ceiling another coat.'

Her voice was brisk, but her eyes were soft. Derek was well satisfied as he went upstairs.

Annie Willis was visiting Margaret at the hospital, so they were able to work on without a break. It was late when they put their brushes away, but there was still more to do.

'I'll come round in the morning,' Charlotte promised.

'On condition you let me take you out for a meal,' Derek smiled.

'I've a better idea. I'll cook for us both. We shouldn't be too late finishing here.'

'Sounds ideal.' Derek held her as she prepared to leave. His kisses showered her face. 'I'll bring the wine.'

As he released her, he added: 'Try not to worry about Holly. She's eighteen and a married woman. You did all you could.'

As Holly Johnston stepped from the bus she caught sight of herself in a shop window.

Throughout the journey she had been wondering what she would say to Rose. Had Charlotte told the truth? Was Rose ill?

Holly couldn't imagine the plump, cosy woman she had loved in any way but the one she remembered. She told herself that once they were together everything would be all right.

But she couldn't go looking the way she did. Holly decided to cash her cheque and find the charity shop Charlotte had mentioned before making her way to the Elmview Tea Room.

It was a different Holly who finally walked into the cafe. She wore a pretty summer dress. A brown jacket and white sandals completed the picture. Even the shabby rucksack was hidden in a large hold-all.

Holly looked round doubtfully. The cafe was empty. Was there no-one serving?

She was sitting at an empty table, checking the address when Marion Formby came up.

'Sorry! Have you been waiting long? What can I get you?'

'Nothing!' Holly burst out, fear building up inside her. She had expected see Rose, to be recognised and welcomed.

'I want to see Auntie Rose.' The old familiar name slipped out. 'I thought she was here.'

Marion looked at her, realising her face was familiar. So this was the child her employer had talked about so much.

Rose had told Marion about her decision not to get in touch with Holly. Marion was convinced she was wrong. The older woman needed someone to care. Only Marion knew how Rose dreaded the future; how she feared for what little sight she had left.

Now the decision was hers, and she could not send Holly away.

'Mrs West has been at the hospital having some treatment. She is resting at the moment. I'll take you up and you can wait till she wakes.'

Marion led the way upstairs, but there was an urgent call from the cafe.

'Wait in the sitting room until you hear her move,' she whispered as she turned to leave.

But the door of the darkened bedroom was open. Holly went in.

Holly stood staring at the still form. Even though the curtains were drawn and Rose West was asleep, Holly could see the changes. The grey hair; the bones revealed where the plumpness had wasted away.

'Oh, Auntie Rose,' she whispered. 'I'll never leave you again. Not until you're well. I love you so much.'

Somehow the intensity of her feelings penetrated

the light sleep of the woman in the bed. She opened her eyes.

Holly bent over, taking her hand.

'It's me, Auntie Rose. I've come to take care of you.'

'Holly!'

For a brief second there was joy in Rose's voice. Then, as sleep receded she sat up, remembering.

'Holly Webster! You're not Holly Webster – you're Holly Johnston. You've a husband. Go back to him. I don't need you here. I don't want you. Go away.'

If Rose had been herself her words would have been less harsh, but her sudden waking from sleep, and her resolution not to be a burden to Holly combined to make her voice harsh and abrupt.

'Didn't you hear me? I told you to go.'

Holly backed away from the bed, her eyes wide with disbelief. Once again her world had fallen apart. Rose West did not want her.

Outside she sank into a heap on the stairs. What was she to do now?

Holly wasn't aware of the passing of time as she sat on the stairs. The bend hid her from curious eyes as the pain of rejection flooded over her. She had been so sure about Rose.

Finally she rose unsteadily to her feet, but instead of going downstairs she walked in the sitting-room. At least she would see where Rose West lived, and know she was comfortable.

Then Holly saw the photograph album. It lay open on the sideboard. Staring up at her was a picture of herself and Rose; happy, arms round each other as they shared a laughter-filled moment.

Slowly Holly turned the pages. As all the memories

flooded back, she realised the album was well thumbed. It must have been looked at many times. So Auntie Rose still thought about the past, and their lovely times together.

Yet she had sent her away. Why?

Standing looking at the pictures of Rose as she used to be, Holly remembered all the other times she had been faced with making a decision. She had always taken the easy way out, run away from difficulties. Now she had a choice.

She could do as Rose West had told her, and walk out. Or she could stay and find the courage to face Rose again.

For a few minutes Holly fought a battle with herself. Then she took off her coat and went into the kitchen. With quiet deliberation she filled the kettle, and found a tray, cups and saucers. Then she carried it in to Rose West.

Rose was lying back on her pillows.

'I thought I told you to go,' she said brusquely.

'I know, but it has been a long morning and I needed a drink,' Holly answered calmly. 'I thought you might like one as well.'

She put the tray on a table and sat on the bed.

'And—' she forced a smile '— I saw the album.'

Rose looked at her warily.

'We had some lovely summers, didn't we, Auntie Rose? Remember how we used to spend too long on the beach and you would have to dash back to get the guests' meals on time?'

Rose nodded, and placed a hand on Holly's.

'Yes, love, I remember. But that is all in the past. We have to face things as they are now, not as we would

75

like them to be.'

Both of them looked down at Rose's hand. It was so thin and white. Holly covered it with her own.

'Let me stay, Auntie Rose, please! Oh, I know I haven't kept in touch, but I've thought about you such a lot.

'It was you I came to Baynton to find. When you weren't there I just went to pieces. Charlotte helped me, but it was you I really wanted.'

Holly gazed appealingly at the older woman. She had seen the careful way Rose held her cup and how she fumbled for the saucer. Rose needed her, but how was she to convince her that she wasn't offering to stay out of pity?

Perhaps it was her new feeling of determination to stand up to her problems that made Holly choose the right words.

'I need you, Auntie. I need you so much.'

Rose saw again the child she had cared for, saw the pleading eyes, and suddenly, for the first time in months, she herself felt needed. As though, restricted as she was, she could help somebody.

But she was still uncertain.

'Holly, what about your husband? You're so young; you have your own life.'

'No, I need time. I'll tell you about it one day, but for now, can't we just be together? Help each other?'

'Holly, I always said that my home was yours. That is still true. If you really want to stay I'll be glad to have you. Now go into the sitting-room while I dress. Then I'll take you downstairs and introduce you to Marion Formby. She can always make use of an extra pair of hands.'

The two women smiled at each other. They were still a little uncertain, but each knew the other cared. And that the changes the years had brought, would, eventually, bring them even closer.

The next day, Charlotte sang as she prepared a meal for herself and Derek.

She still missed Holly, but a telephone call from Scarborough explaining that she was staying with Rose West – and a stammered apology for her hasty words, had set her mind at rest about her young friend.

Charlotte had left Derek putting the finishing touches to his mother's kitchen. She had enjoyed their two days working together. They had recaptured the friendly ease they had always enjoyed in each other's company. Her eyes were soft as she added the finishing touches to the table. Wineglasses, candles —

She was standing back admiring her work when the bell rang. Derek was early! She opened the door, teasing words about skimping the job hovering on her lips. It wasn't Derek.

Bill Menzies stood there, watching the changing expressions on Charlotte's face.

'Bill! I was expecting—' Charlotte stopped, suddenly realising how pleased she was to see him. 'This is a lovely surprise. Do come in.'

Bill took her hands, and she looked up at him, suddenly feeling an unexpected tightness round her heart. She had forgotten how gentle his eyes could be, how strong his grip.

Slowly he bent towards her and she felt the pressure of his lips.

Then the telephone rang and she drew back. The moment slipped away as she turned and picked up the receiver. Beryl Burton's agitated voice carried clearly along the line.

'Charlotte, thank goodness you're in. Listen. I've to go into hospital tonight.'

'But you said next week!'

'I know, but something's gone wrong. Oh, nothing to worry about. It will soon be put right. I haven't told Doctor Wade yet. He's a dear, but he is getting on a bit and is easily flummoxed. You can go into the surgery in the morning, can't you? About eight-thirty?'

'But, Beryl, I—'

'Charlotte, you promised! You can't let me down.'

'No, I can't,' Charlotte said slowly.

Her eyes went to where Bill stood, his face inscrutable as he listened to their conversation.

'I'll be there in the morning. And, Beryl, I hope all goes well for you.'

Slowly she hung up the receiver.

'Bill, I'm sorry. It's only part-time. I don't know how long you can stay, but we will be able to have time together when—'

'When you have time,' Bill interrupted, all the intimacy of the previous few minutes shattered.

'And all this.' He gestured to the table. 'Is it for this Holly you were telling me about?'

Suddenly Charlotte resented his tone, and the fact that he was making her feel guilty about helping Dr Wade. She shook her head.

'Holly left yesterday to stay with a friend. I'm expecting Derek Gregson. We've been painting his mother's kitchen, and I left him to finish off. Please

78

excuse me, I must check the oven.'

In the kitchen Charlotte leaned against the door, giving herself time to collect her thoughts. Why was it she always said the wrong things to Bill?

Slowly she went back into the living-room. Bill was standing by the door.

'Oh, you're not leaving? There's enough food for an army. Please stay.' She hesitated. 'And Bill, I'm glad you came.'

'Are you, Charlotte?'

Bill Menzies had been on the point of giving up. Now he hesitated. He had come here, determined to tell Charlotte how he felt about her. He wouldn't be able to do that if he walked out.

'Right! Anything I can do to help?'

The chicken, in a rich, creamy sauce was delicious, and the fresh fruit salad a perfect finish. But as Charlotte put out cheese and biscuits, she knew the meal had been a failure.

Oh, the two men had talked, but the conversation had been stilted, forced. Even the excellent wine Derek had brought had failed to help matters.

'So your mother is improving?' Bill was asking as she carried the tray in.

'Yes, she should be coming home any time. They'll probably tell me when this evening.

'There's still a long way to go. She'll have to stay in bed a lot and be very careful.'

Charlotte heard the worry in his voice and smiled at him.

'Don't worry, Derek. The district nurse will call regularly and Annie Willis will help. And you know I'm always here if you need me.'

Soon afterwards Derek rose. The evening he had been looking forward to had fallen flat. Having to go to the hospital was a good excuse for leaving.

'I'll ring you if there is any news,' he told Charlotte. Then, knowing Bill was watching, he bent over and kissed her lips.

Looking up at him, Charlotte saw the old mischief in his eyes, and couldn't keep the merriment out of her voice as she turned back to Bill.

'Look, you've been cooped up most of the day. How about a walk? Then you can tell me how the work at Chanlea is going.'

'I'll help you wash up first,' Bill told her.

'Oh, no! I'll do them in the morning.'

'You're a working girl in the morning,' Bill reminded her, aware of his stiffness after Derek's light-heartedness.

'I'll still deal with them tomorrow,' Charlotte insisted stubbornly. She was filled with the urge to get away from the remnants of the disastrous meal. 'Have you a jacket in the car?'

Once down by the sea she hesitated. One way led to the cliffs, where she and Derek always walked, and where she had seen Holly on the beach. She turned the other way and took the path down to the seashore and on to the street winding through the town.

The waves were a soft, gentle ripple; the sands firm, clean washed. The gulls mewed overhead and the seaweed popped beneath their feet.

Charlotte drew deep, refreshing breaths, and was aware of Bill doing the same. Inevitably their hands linked, and Charlotte smiled up at him.

'How are things in London?' she asked.

80

So Bill told her what he hoped to achieve remodelling the grounds of the old house. As he talked his voice became alive, eager. Charlotte looked up at him. How quickly they had grown together again, she thought, now they were alone.

They stopped at an old hotel by the beach and sat in a small, secluded arbour and drank long cool drinks. The sun was dipping behind the skyline when they rose to leave.

On the way back they paused, watching the last shafts of orange vanish behind the purple velvet of the night sky. Bill held Charlotte in the circle of his arms.

Slowly his lips found hers. This time there were no interruptions. Their kiss was long and lingering, and when they drew apart there was wonder in both their hearts.

'Charlotte, I have to go back to London at the weekend. Come back with me?'

'Bill, I can't—'

'You can – if you want to enough. Can't you see I love you?' he went on. 'I want you with me. Can you look at me and tell me you don't feel the same way?'

Again his lips found hers, and again she responded. Her arms pulled him down to her as her hands caressed the back of his neck

'Now tell me you don't love me?' he demanded.

'I didn't say I don't love you.' She sighed. 'But you must give me more time. I have other commitments. I can't just walk out on everyone.'

'But you can walk out on me—'

He released her with a suddenness that left her trembling.

'Everyone else comes first. This doctor fellow;

Derek; his mother; Holly! Oh, yes. Charlotte will help out.

'I'm sorry, but I can't wait in a queue! I can't take second, third, fourth place in your life.'

'Bill, please –'

But he was already walking away. Stumbling in the half light she hurried after him. When she caught him up, apart from putting a steadying hand on her arm over the rough ground, he walked apart, silent.

It was only when they reached his car that he looked at her.

'Come inside, Bill – please,' she pleaded. 'We have to talk.'

He shook his head. 'I think it's all been said.

'Oh, Charlotte, I came with such high hopes. You're the only girl that has really mattered to me. I was so sure you cared enough. I was wrong.'

His voice shook as he went on: 'I don't know what you want out of life, but whatever it is, I hope you find it.'

He reached out and caressed her face, gently; so achingly gently. Then he was in the car, driving away.

Charlotte groped her way into the house. Bill, she thought. Oh, Bill, what have I done?

Seven

Charlotte spent a wakeful night and, next morning, slept through the alarm.

A hurried cup of coffee and a quick slice of toast did little to settle her taut nerves. There was no time to ring Bill Menzies and the thought of their parting the night before was uppermost in Charlotte's mind as she hurried round to Dr Wade's.

Charlotte and Beryl had planned to have a few days working together, but the receptionist's sudden departure had made that impossible.

Beryl had tried to leave everything in order, but Charlotte found the work strange and rather confusing. At the health centre there had been computers with all the patients' history neatly stored away. Here, she found Beryl's filing system confusing and hard to follow.

Elderly Doctor Wade, so understanding with his patients, was difficult to work for. Charlotte was there as his receptionist, and as far as he was concerned should be able to carry on just as Beryl had done. When he asked for notes or other particulars, he expected them there, immediately.

It was after twelve o'clock when the last patient left. Charlotte still had files to put away and medical supplies to clear.

'Leave that for now,' Doctor Wade told her. 'Bring coffee in here for both of us.'

Charlotte would rather have done without the coffee. Her head was throbbing as she carried the tray into the surgery. His old gentle smile was back.

'You look tired, Charlotte. Have I been a bit rough on you? I should have remembered everything was new to you. Sorry, my dear.'

Charlotte relaxed slightly, but remained silent. Doctor Wade, slowly stirring his coffee, obviously had more to say.

'I had a telephone call from the hospital,' he told her. 'Margaret Gregson is being discharged this afternoon.'

Charlotte heard the slight, underlying anxiety in his voice.

'Surely that's good news, Doctor? Or is there something you haven't told us?'

'No, nothing like that. It's just that, well, I know Margaret. She isn't going to find it easy to slow down. I'm not at all sure she realises how important the hospital's instructions are.'

'In what way?' Charlotte asked.

'Diet mainly, and proper rest. Not easy for someone as independent as Margaret. She's going to need someone around to keep an eye on her. Her son did ask me about a nurse, but that would be making too much of an invalid of her.'

'You're asking me to help?'

The old man sighed. 'Only as Margaret's friend, not as her doctor. Margaret trusts you, she'd take notice.'

Charlotte stood up.

'I'll be there if she needs me. After all that's why I came home in the first place.'

If the doctor noticed the trace of bitterness in her voice, he ignored it.

'Thanks, Charlotte, and thanks for helping me out as well. It's afternoon surgery tomorrow, so you could finish clearing up in the morning. I'll try and be a little more patient tomorrow,' he finished with a smile.

When Charlotte arrived home the first thing she did was ring Bill Menzies at the hotel. She knew what she would say.

Please, Bill, come round. I'm sorry about last night. We have to talk –

'I'm sorry,' the voice at the other end of the line was saying, 'Mr Menzies checked out this morning.'

Charlotte replaced the receiver. Sinking into a chair she fought back tears of frustration. If only she hadn't slept in! If only she'd made time to ring from the surgery!

She closed her eyes and remembered the night before. The urgency of Bill's kisses, his words of love. How her heart had leapt in response.

Sitting there, in the quiet of her old home, Charlotte at last acknowledged her love for Bill Menzies. At the same time, she faced the fact that she had thrown away any chance of becoming part of his life.

She was not foolish enough to think everything had ended. She would pick up the pieces and carry on. But would she always carry this sense of loss, of happiness thrown away?

Charlotte must have slept, for the ringing of the telephone disturbed her.

'That you, Charlotte?' It was Derek's voice. 'I'm fetching Mother out at three-thirty. I know you've been working, but would you be a dear and come? She will feel better if you're there. Bill as well, of course.'

Charlotte couldn't bear to tell Derek about Bill. She quietly arranged to meet him at the hospital.

Margaret Gregson was pale, but quite talkative. Derek helped her into the front seat of the car he had hired for his stay in Baynton.

'Now what have you done with this young man of yours?' she asked Charlotte as Derek manoeuvred the car out of the busy grounds. 'Derek thought he would be coming with you.'

'Bill's back in London. We – well, we had a talk last night and I think everything's over.'

Charlotte tried to keep her voice light. She was glad of the back seat, away from her friend's observant eyes.

She didn't see the satisfaction on Margaret's face. If Charlotte had been happy with Bill, she would have wished her well, but now all her old dreams sprang to life again.

Of course, there was Celia from New York to contend with, but with Charlotte coming so much to the house Derek would see a lot of her.

'Thanks, Holly! You pop upstairs now. I'll finish off down here.'

Marion Formby smiled at her new assistant. Holly had soon picked up the run of things, and although a little shy, was pleasant both to the customers and the other staff.

'Tired?' Rose West asked as Holly joined her in the sitting-room.

Holly laughed, shaking her head.

'Not a bit. I enjoy the work.'

'Well, sit down a bit. The coffee's made, and don't tell me I shouldn't have. If you fuss too much, I'll just have to turn you out!'

They smiled at each other. Slowly, after a difficult start, they were regaining their pleasure in each other's company. Conversation, hesitant at first, as each feared intruding on the other's privacy, grew more spontaneous.

Holly's next words came out easily.

'Oh, Auntie Rose! I'm so happy here with you. If only Dad had married someone like you when he was younger. He might have stayed at home more and been there when I needed him. I might never have finished up like this—'

'You mean married to Roger?'

'I think I would have always married Roger eventually, we loved each other so much. But not as I did, a hole-in-the-corner affair. We'd have worked first, saved up. Made a decent home for—'

Holly stopped abruptly, and Rose didn't probe. She knew eventually Holly would talk. Tell her the real trouble.

They sat contentedly in the warmth from the gas fire, and sipped their coffee.

The young man glanced at the slip of paper in his hand and then back at the cafe. It was the place all right. Still he hesitated.

He pushed the paper into his pocket, slung his jacket from one arm to the other and walked inside.

Marion Formby smiled as she walked up to her late customer.

'We're almost closed, but I can manage a snack?'

The young man shook his head, smiling nervously.

'Actually I came hoping to see Holly Johnston. I understand she is living here.'

Marion hesitated, but she had not the right to refuse him.

'I can see if she's in. What name shall I say?'

'It doesn't matter. I just want to talk to her.'

Marion went upstairs.

'Come for coffee?' Rose asked.

'No, thank you.'

Marion thought she had never seen Rose looking so happy. She had a feeling that the young man downstairs was about to disturb that happiness, but she could not have sent him away.

'Someone asking to see you, Holly.'

'Thanks, I'll be right down.'

Holly expected her visitor to be one of the people she had met in the cafe, or perhaps Charlotte.

She turned the bend in the staircase and her heart turned over.

'Roger!'

She wasn't ready for him – not yet. If he hadn't seen her, she would have turned and fled. As their eyes met he walked slowly towards her. Holly, unable to move, waited.

'Holly! Holly,' he repeated, 'we have to talk.'

'I need more time,' she whispered.

Roger took her hands. She didn't pull away, just

looked down at the work roughened hands holding hers, and shook her head.

'You went away,' she murmured. 'I didn't know—'

'I didn't mean to leave you. Please listen. We must find somewhere to talk. I don't want to hurt you any more. Have you a room?'

Holly's eyes were changing. Emotions flickered across her face; disbelief and a hint of fear that tore at Roger's heart.

Holly remembered Rose West. Whatever happened, Rose must not be upset.

'We can't talk here,' she told him. 'I'll get a coat.'

Forcing a lightness to her voice, she went in to Rose.

'You all right? I'm just going for a stroll. I won't be late.'

'That's nice! I'm glad you've found a friend. Don't worry about me. There's a concert on the radio I want to listen to.'

They walked down by the sea. Boats tossed in the harbour. Seagulls swooped round a fishing trawler as its catch was unloaded onto the pier. The sky was still blue, the evening warm and gentle.

It was Roger who spoke first.

'Holly, that morning when I walked out, I didn't mean to stay away. And those things I said, I didn't mean them.'

'But you said them!'

Holly's voice was low, taut with remembered pain.

'You said it was my fault, that I had let our baby die.'

All the agony of those dreadful days flooded back. She crossed her arms and rocked with grief.

'Holly, listen to me! I know it wasn't your fault. I knew it even as I was saying it.'

'But if I'd gone into him, perhaps—'

'Look, love, it was *not* your fault. Nigel was mine as well. If you were even partly to blame, then so was I.

'Oh, Holly, I loved him so much; loved you both so much; and I could do so little for you. I felt such a failure! If only I hadn't lost my job, perhaps if I'd been able to give you more. . . .'

The flow of words came to a ragged halt. Rubbing his hand across his eyes, Roger took a deep, steadying breath before continuing.

'Then the funeral, the tiny coffin. I didn't know anyone could feel like that, as though they were being torn apart. And you were so white, so quiet. You hardly cried. Just looked at me with those huge eyes as though I should be able to help you. Able to bring our baby back.

'I wanted to hold you, to talk, but you seemed so remote, so wrapped up in your own grief, I didn't know how to reach you.

'Don't you see, love, we were both too young? I didn't know how to cope. The inquest, everything seemed to be happening to someone else, not to Roger Johnston.'

Again he paused, but still Holly said nothing. As if fearing the silence he began talking again.

'That last morning, I looked round the space we called a flat, and something seemed to burst in my head. I was twenty-two and that – that shoe box was all I could provide for my wife; the only home my son had known! I'd had such hopes, such plans for us all, and I had to let my anger out. You were there.

'I wanted to know someone else was hurting as much as I was. I didn't stop to think that you were already suffering more than me. I'm sorry. I just don't know what else I can say.'

Roger Johnston wasn't a great talker, but this time it was as though a dam had burst. Words, phrases, emotions had just flowed from him. Now, spent, he sat beside his wife on the low sea wall and stared out into the darkening blue of the sky.

Holly stirred, and reached out, touching his arm. Then she drew away, as though the brief contact had hurt her.

'Why didn't you come back?' Her voice was low. 'You said you didn't mean to leave me.'

'I didn't. I just walked round and went into a transport cafe for a cup of tea. I got talking to a lorry driver and hitched a lift to Leeds.

'I stayed in a hostel and did odd jobs in the warehouse where the bloke worked. Last week the manager offered me a job.'

'How did you find me?'

'When I had the chance of regular work I hitched a lift to Bristol. The landlady said you'd gone, but she gave me Charlotte Saunders' address. Miss Saunders gave me this one.'

He turned and looked at Holly.

'What I said earlier, about Nigel. Were you listening?'

'Yes, but I can't talk about it, not yet. I could have done then, back in the flat, only you wouldn't listen.

'Now? Well I don't think I'm the same person. I've changed. I'm not sure how, but I have to find out.'

'Just tell me one thing.' Roger spoke softly. 'Is your father behind this? Has he told you not to have anything more to do with me?'

'Dad! he doesn't even know we've separated. I tried to get in touch with him after Nigel was born and couldn't. I haven't bothered since. I don't suppose there was a letter from him in Bristol?'

'No – it all seemed to be junk mail. I just threw it out.'

Holly shrugged. 'I didn't think there would be. I suppose I'll write eventually. Auntie Rose seems to think I should.'

She looked at him and Roger's heart contracted. What had he done? He had loved Holly since he was a schoolboy. Now she was looking at him as though she had never seen him before.

Gently he took her hand and drew her to her feet.

'It's getting chilly. Let's walk a bit.'

So they walked along the Marine Drive. They didn't hold hands; they didn't talk. It was Holly who suggested they turn back.

As they came back to where Holly had to branch away, they leaned against the rail. Now the tide was out. There was only the gentle lapping of the waves over the almost deserted beach.

'Is there a bus back to Leeds?'

Holly's voice was that of a polite stranger, making conversation.

'Yes, but I've plenty of time.'

He turned to face her, suddenly aware of all the things he had intended saying.

'Holly! Please – won't you come—'

'No! I know what you're trying to say, but I can't. I've just started a new life. I have to find out if it's what I want. And there's Auntie Rose. She needs me.'

'But we have to see each other again. You're still my wife. I care about you. I love you,' he added slowly. 'I always have, but I've never known you like this.'

'I told you, I've changed. I think it is called maturing, growing up.'

'At least say you'll meet me. Give me a chance to know the new Holly.'

'I suppose you have the right. Auntie Rose would like to meet you, but that's all it will be,' she added, turning to look at him. 'Just a meeting.'

'Very well.' He nodded agreement, wondering at the change in the girl he married. Where was the young girl who had always needed him, listened to him?

'Come to tea on Sunday. Round about four o'clock. Now I'd better be getting back. I don't like leaving Auntie Rose too long.'

Their leave-taking outside the cafe was brief. A quick touching of hands, and Holly was gone.

Roger Johnston's thoughts were in a turmoil as he walked to the bus. He had been so sure Holly would come back to him. If only he hadn't said all those dreadful things. If only Nigel had lived.

Meanwhile Holly, peeping round Rose West's door found her awake.

'Had a nice walk?'

Holly, suddenly weary, sat on the bed. She was not yet ready for explanations. Roger had brought back all the memories. Memories she hoped had softened, begun to heal. Now they were raw, torn open. She needed time before she talked to Rose.

'Yes, thank you. It's a lovely evening. Anything you need?'

Rose noticed the hesitation, but said nothing. Holly would talk when she was ready.

Eight

It was Friday evening and Charlotte had just finished her third day as Doctor Wade's receptionist. Doctor Wade smiled at her as he walked through reception on his way out.

'No surgery tomorrow. You'll enjoy some time off. I'm sorry if I've been a bit short with you. You've done well, and I appreciate it.'

It was a pleasant evening and Charlotte decided to walk round and see Margaret Gregson. There was a surprise for her when she walked into Margaret's sitting-room. Holly Johnston rose to greet her, laughing at her friend's obvious surprise.

'Marion thought I should have the afternoon off, I rang you, but forgot you were one of the world's workers,' she teased. 'So I went to the hospital instead to see Margaret and she had been discharged. So here I am.'

They chatted for a while, entertaining Margaret with stories about the cafe and the funny things the patients had said, then went into the kitchen to make a drink.

'I hope I didn't do wrong, giving Roger your address,' Charlotte began. 'Only I was just dashing off to the surgery or I might have rung you.'

'No, it was all right. We had to meet sometime. We talked.'

'And — ?' Charlotte prompted.

'We just talked,' she repeated.'He's coming to tea on Sunday.'

There was an uncertain note in her voice, but there was no time for more talk, Margaret was calling to them.

'Here, have a slice of this delicious chocolate cake Holly brought me.'

Margaret pushed the box over and Charlotte looked at her in mock despair.

'Margaret! You haven't — ?'

'Only the tiniest bit,' Margaret admitted sheepishly. 'After all, it was a present!'

Charlotte shook her head. Doctor Wade had been right when he said Margaret Gregson wouldn't take kindly to her diet. Somehow they would have to make her realise how vital it was that she stick to it.

When Holly left, Margaret admitted she felt tired. She still looked frail but as Charlotte was about to suggest an early night for her, the telephone rang.

Derek, who was working upstairs on some papers from New York, came down to answer it.

'Celia! This is a pleasant surprise! Where are you? Rome?'

Margaret pulled a face at Charlotte.

'Don't like her,' she muttered.

Charlotte grinned at her mutinous expression.

'You don't even know her,' she whispered.

'I still don't like her.' Derek went on talking.

'No, love! I can't possibly fly out. – Why? Well, Mother's home for one thing. Goodness knows what she'd get up to on her own.'

'Hear-hear.' His mother winked at Charlotte.

'And I'm working, even if it is by remote control. But we do have a spare room, and Baynton isn't quite the back of beyond.

'That was Celia,' Derek informed them as he came in to the room. 'She's in Rome, had some good sales, apparently. Leaves for Switzerland tomorrow, then it's Paris and London.'

'A lot of silly nonsense,' declared Margaret. 'After all, you can only wear one dress at a time. A waste of money, I call it, but I suppose it's all right for someone without the brains for anything else.'

Charlotte and Derek burst out laughing.

'Subject closed,' Derek decided. 'Now I'm going to fetch us a takeaway.'

'No, you're not!' Margaret told him firmly. 'Annie Willis is coming in later and we'll have supper together. You're going to go upstairs, get out of those awful jeans and take Charlotte out for a meal.'

Derek drove to a charming hotel near Thornton Dale. They lingered, talking with the ease of old friends.

There was still some daylight left when they had finished their meal and Derek drove into the beautiful Forge Valley. The sun was dipping golden behind the trees, lending extra enchantment to the lovely valley below.

As Derek parked the car it seemed the most natural thing in the world for his arm to circle Charlotte's shoulders, and for her head to rest against the soft texture of his shirt. Slowly, with infinite gentleness, his lips sought hers.

Charlotte, wrapped in the magic of the night, wound her arms round him, drawing him close. His kisses became more demanding and she found herself responding with a passion she had thought alien to her nature.

Only when she felt his hands moving over her body did sanity return. She eased herself away, taking his hand and raising it to her lips to ease the rejection.

'No, Derek! Please.'

'But Charlotte, I care about you so much. I need you—'

Charlotte, as so often in their younger years was the wiser of the two.

'Derek, we were carried away by the moonlight, and the mood. We'd better go.'

'I think – I was going to ask you to marry me.' He tipped her face so he could look into her eyes.

'And I might have said "yes", and then we could both have been sorry. You have to see Celia and see how you feel.'

'And you? Do you have to see Bill?'

'No, Bill has walked out of my life. Take me home now. It has been a wonderful evening, all of it. And I mean all,' she told him softly.

That night Charlotte relived the evening.

I care about you – Derek had said, not *I love you. I can't go on without you.* She remembered his kisses and her own instinctive response.

But when she slept she dreamed of walking beside another man, a man who brought with him the

98

freshness of the outdoors, and whose shoulders were firm beneath the roughness of a worn tweed jacket.

Marion Formby was pleased to see Holly looking brighter after her visit to Margaret Gregson.

'And how is the old lady?'

'She isn't really old. She was quite bright and perky, but somehow I didn't think she was all that good.'

Holly walked slowly up to Rose West's sitting-room. She knew it was time to talk.

Rose had drawn the curtains so she could see the blurred outline of the television better. Holly switched the set off, but left the curtains, glad of the semi-darkness.

She sat on the rug, her head resting against Rose's knee. Rose, sensing Holly had something to say, waited.

'Auntie, the other night, when I went out, it wasn't with a friend.' Her voice trembled. 'It was with my husband, Roger.'

'I guessed as much,' Rose said quietly. 'How did it go?'

'It was awful. Like tearing open an old wound. You see, we had a baby, a little boy.'

This time Rose was still. Her little Holly, a mother?

'Holly, you have a child?'

'I *had* a child. His name was Nigel. He was so beautiful. His tiny fingers would cling to mine, and he was just beginning to smile. I loved him so much.

'But Roger lost his job, and it was so difficult managing. I got so that I didn't care about the flat, or how I looked. As long as Nigel was all right I let everything else go.

'Then one day I met a neighbour. Florence Young, just as she was going into her flat. She looked so smart and happy. She told me she had just retired and held out a bottle of wine.

"Have a drink and wish me luck,"she said.

'I put the wine on the table and it looked so out of place with a huge red bow round its neck. For the first time in ages I looked round. The place was neglected, grubby. There was washing draped all over. It was two flights down to the drying ground. Toys, newspapers, and I hadn't even washed the dishes.

'I saw myself in the mirror and thought how well I matched the flat. My hair was awful and I'd just pulled on old jeans and a sloppy top, the first things I could find.

'By the time Roger came home I had tidied the flat and prettied myself up. I saw his face change as though all the frustration had been wiped away.

'We put Nigel to bed together, then went through our pockets and found enough change for a take-away.

'It was as it had been when we were first married. We were suddenly happy and close again. I did think about Nigel when we went to bed but he was a good baby and often slept through.

'We'd had the wine – and Roger was loving me. I didn't go in to him.

'The next morning we overslept. When I did go in, he – he – '

Blindly she turned to Rose. The older woman folded her in her arms making no effort to stem the tears.

Rose guessed rightly that these were the first real tears Holly had shed, and Rose knew that only by releasing the pain that had built up inside her, would the process of true healing begin.

Later, Holly looked up at her, her eyes old, her voice barely a whisper.

'After the funeral Roger walked out. He said it was my fault. That I had let our baby die.'

Her voice died on a quiver of pain, and Rose could find no words of comfort. Gently she cupped the tear-stained face in her hands.

'He was wrong, my dear. We all say things we don't mean when we're upset – unhappy. You were both so young. Roger couldn't cope with his own grief, let alone comfort you in yours.'

And neither can I, she thought sadly as she stroked the tumble of hair on her lap.

'I waited and waited, and he didn't come home. I didn't bother going out. I just stayed in the flat and wondered why I had to live.

'Then one day I thought of you and how happy we used to be. I don't know how I got to Baynton, but you weren't there. Then I met Charlotte, and, well, you know the rest.'

'And now you have talked to Roger?'

'I didn't feel anything. I'm not sure I even want to see him on Sunday. I just want to stay here with you.'

'And I want you, love. But Roger is your husband. You must give your marriage a chance. Please, Holly.'

Holly was silent for a few minutes. It was a promise she could not make lightly. Then she looked up at Rose.

'I'll try, Auntie,' she said softly. 'Now let me help you to bed. Then I'll read to you for a while.'

Rose West looked up at Holly's husband and liked what she saw. His handshake was firm, his smile gentle, caring. Only when she looked into his eyes did she read the doubts, the uncertainties that were still there, but she also saw the depth of love in them as they rested on his young wife, and knew instinctively that Holly's future would be safe with Roger Johnston.

Holly had feared the visit would be strained, uncomfortable, but she was wrong. Holly listened to her young husband conversing easily, and knew he was no longer the immature boy she had married. Somewhere during the last few weeks he had grown up.

How would she feel if they had just met? I could care about him, she thought, I could care a lot. Her eyes met his and she smiled, unaware that her eyes mirrored her thoughts and raised anew his hopes that soon they would be together again.

When they were left alone Rose leaned towards Roger.

'She needs time,' she said gently. 'Losing a child like that—' She shook her head, knowing she herself could only guess at the extent of Holly's grief.

'I do love Holly, Auntie Rose. I will make her happy, if she will give me another chance.'

Rose liked the easy way he used Holly's name for her.

'I think she will, but don't try to rush her. As I said time has a way of sorting our lives out.'

In the shelter of the cafe door Roger pulled Holly to him, and bent to kiss her; she didn't return the kiss, but neither did she pull away. She watched him as he left, and long after he was out of sight, Holly still stood, knowing his kiss had done nothing for her.

Rose was already in bed when she went back to the sitting room, and Holly curled up in an armchair. There was still light from outside, and the gas fire sent flickering shadows about the room. Holly let her thoughts drift, and strangely it was her childhood that filled her mind.

She thought about her father. Was it her fault that things had gone wrong? Sitting there she remembered the happy times. The times he had suddenly taken her on unexpected outings, laughed with her and teased her. The time he decorated her room just as she asked – but always he had retreated. Always there had been his fossils, his queer collection of old pottery and things from the past.

How happy she had been when he had shared the first few days of the holidays with her at Baynton, but beneath her pleasure, teasing away was the knowledge that before very long he would walk away.

How did he feel now? She had been determined to wait until he tried to find her, but he hadn't approved of her marriage, and he had his pride too. She would write to him once more, not tonight, but in a day or two.

The July sun was hot on the tarmac when Celia Hammerton stepped from the plane at Heathrow.

Usually Celia was on top of the world during her rounds of the famous fashion houses. She had a flair for fashion, for knowing what each buyer wanted to see, what the store in New York that employed her would be able to sell. But this trip had fallen flat. Her bubbly enthusiasm for her work had been missing.

Once in the privacy of her hotel bedroom, she slipped into a loose housecoat, crossed over to the drinks cabinet and poured herself a long, cool glass of orange. Then she stretched out on the bed and reviewed the past couple of weeks.

She had been to Rome, Venice and Paris, but there was none of her usual elation. Ruefully she admitted the reason. Derek Gregson.

Celia had been sure he would fly over and join her in Paris. Certain that the attraction that had been so strong in New York would surface again. Now, she went thoughtfully over her telephone conversations with him.

His mother was obviously improving. He had said he didn't want to leave her, but she had friends and a nurse going in. She also had Charlotte! Charlotte his childhood sweetheart. Celia had never known jealousy, she had always been confident, assured, but now — .

Almost she dialled Derek's number, but refrained. Her inclinations were to rush straight to Baynton, but she knew she had to attend to her business commitments first. Celia had struggled up from nothing and was determined not to slip back.

That evening she had a dinner appointment with a designer whose sketches seemed perfect for modern trends.

When she was ready she stood in front of the mirror. Tall and slender. Soft, almost platinum blonde hair piled high and caught in place by a red butterfly clasp which toned perfectly with her red sheath dress. A cream jacket was flung carelessly across her shoulders.

Picking up her evening bag she made her way to the hotel foyer. A week at the most and she would go to Baynton.

There was a lilt to her voice as she gave the taxi driver instructions.

'Surprise, surprise!'

Charlotte Saunders looked up as Derek Gregson walked into Dr Wade's surgery.

'Still busy?' he asked.

'Almost through. Just these files. Doctor Wade's just left.'

'Yes, I met him. He was asking about Mother.'

'Well, you could give him a good report.' Charlotte turned the key in the filing cabinet and looked at him. 'Anyway he sees her every week still, surely.'

'Oh yes, and physically she is improving. Slips up still with her diet and pills, but she is even coming to terms with that. It's just something. You know,' he added thoughtfully, 'it's as though Mother doesn't want to get well, really well I mean.'

'Of course she doesn't, you clot,' Charlotte felt like answering. 'If she does she's afraid her only son will depart again to New York and she will be left alone in that big house.'

But of course, she couldn't say anything like that. Any decisions about his future would have to come from Derek himself, so she smiled and asked him how the garden, his latest project, was coming on.

'Come back and see,' he suggested. 'Mum was saying we hadn't seen much of you this last week or two.'

'You wouldn't be wanting a bit of help, by any

chance,' Charlotte teased, but Derek only grinned.

'Well I wouldn't say no, as you know I am not the world's most enthusiastic gardener.'

Margaret Gregson greeted Charlotte with obvious pleasure. They had already had their evening meal, so after a chat, Derek and Charlotte went out into the garden.

As Charlotte had predicted she was soon wearing an old pair of Margaret's gloves and cutting back the overgrowth. She didn't mind though. After being cooped up in the surgery and listening to patients' troubles the fresh air felt good.

Derek began to sing as he knelt by the border planting out heather plants he had just bought. Charlotte joined in and in the house Annie Willis and Margaret Gregson smiled.

'Has Charlotte said how Beryl Burton's baby is?' Annie asked.

'Doing well, after a shaky start. Charlotte has been to see them.'

'And does Beryl still plan to return to work?' Annie asked slowly.

'I suppose so, but surely that won't be for a few months yet. Mothers don't leave young babies.'

'Now they do.' Annie's eyes were grave as she looked at her friend. 'Especially when there is someone like Beryl's mother ready to look after the child. Remember Beryl and her husband have just moved into a new house. I expect they had counted on two wages coming in.

'You have to face it, Margaret. Charlotte will be returning to London eventually. She can't stay here indefinitely without a job, and there isn't much in her line in Baynton, if she did want to stay.'

'Oh, Annie. I know all that! Don't you think it's on my mind all the time? And Derek, so busy getting the house to rights. Redecorated throughout. A cleaner coming once a week as well as the home help, and now the garden.'

Both women were silent for a while, their eyes on Charlotte. Derek, still kneeling, was out of sight but the none-too-musical sound of his voice overpowered Charlotte's as the strains of 'Little Old Lady' came in through the open window.

'He will leave me again, Annie. The last time I could smile and wave him off, but now—'

'Oh, if only he and Charlotte—'

Annie looked at her friend. She heard the heartbreak in her voice but there was little she could say. Few young people settled in Baynton.

'I thought there was another girl, Celia?'

'And I hope was is the proper word!' Margaret Gregson sighed. 'Didn't care for the sound of her at all. Now how about getting the cards out?'

It was getting dusk when Charlotte and Derek finally came in. Annie Willis was just leaving, and remarked how nice it was to see the garden looking cared for. Derek laughed ruefully.

'It's all right getting it nice, but who's going to keep it that way?'

Across the room Annie's eyes met Margaret's. Impulsively Annie went back and leaning over, kissed the still frail-looking woman goodnight.

Charlotte was in the bathroom washing her hands when the telephone rang. As she came downstairs Derek was replacing the receiver.

'It's Celia Hammerton,' he said blankly. 'She's at Yeaden Airport and wants me to pick her up.'

'At this time of night? Most inconsiderate. I hope you told her to get a taxi and go to an hotel—'

'I did nothing of the sort, Mother, and you know it. I guessed she would be in London soon, and half intended to join her for a night or two. But it will be fun showing her how the other half live.'

He grinned mischievously, and there was no doubt in the minds of the two women that he was looking forward to seeing Celia.

'Actually she tried to book in to an hotel in Scarborough, but they were full until tomorrow. It is the busiest time of the season after all.

'It's just – Charlotte, I can't leave Mother alone. Can you stay until we get back?'

The last thing Charlotte wanted was to be present when Derek brought this unknown girl home, but he was right. Margaret couldn't be left, so she nodded.

'I'll wait.'

Derek changed quickly into a clean shirt and sweater.

'Mother,' he said quietly as he bent over to give her a hug. 'You will be nice to her, won't you?'

'I'm always courteous to guests in my house,' Margaret Gregson said stiffly.

As they heard the car drive away, Margaret stood up.

'Well, it's past my bedtime and I'm not waiting up for any Celia. What will you do love?'

'Me? I'll help you to bed. Oh, yes, I know you can manage, but it is nice to be cosseted sometimes, then I'll put a couple of bottles in the spare bed and check

108

the room.'

'Thanks love. Has Derek talked to you about Celia?' Margaret added wistfully as Charlotte took the pins from her hair.

'No, not really. But don't worry, Margaret. Derek would never let you down and he's too sensible to make the wrong choice.'

'But not sensible enough to make the right one,' Margaret answered. 'How about you? Heard from that Bill lately?'

'No! I told you that's all over. Bill Menzies and I didn't see things in the same light. It was better to finish when we did.'

Charlotte turned and went into the kitchen. Margaret lay back on her pillows. Her pills always made her sleepy.

It was almost two o'clock, when Charlotte, drowsing in a chair, heard Derek's car.

Celia, even after the journey looked immaculate in a dark green trouser suit and cerise blouse.

Charlotte had to use the word beautiful, as she looked at the girl she had thought about so much. But nice as well, her mind added as Celia smiled and held out a hand.

'We have spoken, on the telephone. I'm sorry if I've kept you up, I did try an hotel but—'

'That's all right. I have the kettle on, if you'd like a hot drink. I think Mrs Gregson is asleep—'

'Well you think wrong!' Margaret's door opened and she walked slowly into the room. Slowly, because pride had prevented her using her stick, just as pride had made her put on her best housecoat, and a touch of make up, despite the hour.

She took Celia's outstretched hand and then turned to her son.

'Show your friend up to her room, then run Charlotte home. She's had a long day and has to work tomorrow.'

Celia's colour rose at the implied criticism and she looked at Derek rather ruefully as he deposited her luggage in the bedroom.

'She's okay really,' he told her. 'Just make yourself at home. I won't be long.'

Celia looked round the room. Charlotte had put a couple of roses in a slender vase. The bed was turned back, warm and inviting, but Celia knew she would have to go downstairs again. When she found Margaret in the kitchen, making tea, she hesitated, but Margaret turned to her.

'Would you carry the tray through, Celia. Derek won't be long and it will keep hot for him. If you'd like to take yours to your room, do so. I'm going back to bed.'

'I will take mine up,' Celia said. 'And Mrs Gregson, thanks for having me – I didn't know what to do when the hotel was full.'

Margaret was tempted to say for a seasoned traveller she soon stuck fast, but resisted.

'You did right to contact Derek,' she said as she made to leave the room. 'His friends are always welcome.'

As she eased herself back into bed, Margaret knew she could not dislike this girl Derek had brought home. Disapprove of her make up, her expensive clothes, yes, but Margaret had seen the warmth in her eyes, heard the uncertainty in her voice, and knew

Celia was not the hard-headed American she had expected.

But neither was she Charlotte, she thought sadly, as she heard Celia going quietly up the stairs.

The next morning Celia came down to the smell of frying bacon and found Derek wielding the frying-pan with practised dexterity. In spite of her protests he insisted on her eating a proper English breakfast, then, unusually hesitant, Celia carried a tray of tea and toast in to her hostess.

Margaret patted the bed, and Celia sat down.

'And what are your plans for today?'

'I'm moving on to the hotel in Scarborough.'

'You don't have to,' Margaret broke in. 'If you would like to stay here—'

Their eyes met and each knew the other's thoughts. Celia shook her head.

'It is very kind of you, but I think it would be better for me to go. Less work for you, I know you've been ill. Thank you all the same,' she smiled.

It was nearly lunch-time when Derek Gregson accompanied Celia to the spacious hotel room over-looking South Bay. Once the porter had left them he walked over to her, and slowly took her in his arms.

'Welcome to Yorkshire,' he said softly. 'You know we've hardly had time to say hello and I'm just beginning to realise how very much I've missed you, Celia Hammerton.'

He bent and his lips roamed her face, her eyes, her cheeks, and finally, her lips. Her arms were round him, drawing him close and when the kiss ended she took his hand, drawing him towards the settee by the window, but he shook his head.

'Don't tempt me! If I'd known you were coming I'd have had a free day, but there are papers I must mail today.

'I'll pick you up around seven, and we'll go out for dinner. Until then—'

Celia could feel the pressure of his lips long after he had left. Why then did she feel uneasy? As Celia hung up her clothes she felt suddenly alone. She had worked hard to reach her present position and her so called friends were those who she had met on the way up, or down.

Now she remembered a girl who had made time to put roses in the room of a girl she didn't know. A girl with a gentle smile.

Charlotte Saunders! She crossed to the telephone.

'Charlotte! I hope you don't mind – it's me! Celia Hammerton. I wondered, well could I come and see you for an hour? I know you go to work — ?'

'Of course you can come. There isn't a surgery this afternoon. Just get a bus to Baynton and. . . .'

Charlotte was thoughtful as she put the receiver down. Why did Celia want to talk to her?

Celia left the hotel and was about to hail a taxi when she remembered Charlotte's instructions. Suddenly she grinned; when in Rome, she told herself as she asked directions to the bus station.

Nine

As Sam Webster read the letter from his daughter, Holly, his surroundings became a blur, he felt a strange coldness creeping though his limbs, a hammering in his head as though his brain refused to accept the words he was reading.

He had a grandson – no, he had had a grandson. For a few short weeks the child had lived, breathed, and he had been unaware of his existence. A fierce resentment against his daughter, who had kept the news from him was his first reaction, but when the hammering in his brain eased, he immediately rejected it.

Holly had written after her marriage, had tried to heal the rift, but he had refused to accept the olive branch. He checked the dates. Nigel, the name felt strange to his ears, had been born while he was away in the Cantabrean Mountains, and Sam had still been there when his grandson's brief life had ended.

For a long time he sat, sharing his daughter's grief, suffering in some part as she had done. He had let his daughter down when she had most needed him.

Looking back he knew he had let her down time and time again, and time and time again as she had done now, Rose West had stepped in and helped. But this —

He groaned and buried his face in his hands. He must go to her, but even as he made the decision his eyes fell on the papers in front of him. His work was just beginning to pay off. Three lectures during the next two weeks and four magazine articles.

Sam knew he had to honour these commitments. Somehow he felt it would in part justify the damage he had done to his daughter. It was the beginning of a dream come true, a dream when he would get paid, well paid to do the work he loved. Then he would have something to offer Holly, something to show Rose West.

Slowly he began to write. Again and again he tried to find the right words, but even then the letter appeared hard and unfeeling, a poor substitute for himself.

Suddenly he stood up, tore the offending sheets of paper across and across. Always there had been something, something he imagined was vital to his welfare, something more important than, first his wife, then Holly, and later Rose West. How often he had walked away and left Holly to be cared for by Rose West. Even now he could hear Rose's quiet voice suggesting he stay a while — .

The urge for freedom had already lost him any chance of sharing for a few hours the brief life of his grandson; his daughter was almost a stranger; and Rose – dear Rose was again caring for Holly.

He sat down. One thing his ramblings had taught

him was patience, that somewhere, in the most unlikely place he could find something precious, something to treasure. Holly had written to him, he must build on that, seek for a share in Holly's life as patiently as he would search for a bit of old pottery, a scrap of anything from the past.

He took a fresh sheet of paper and began to write. Later he would telephone, ask if the lectures could be postponed, the articles submitted at a later date. If not, there would be other opportunities.

Holly read the letter, her eyes stony, her lips tight. So often her father had ignored her. Holly had been too proud to show how much she needed him. Would this time be any different, in spite of his promise? Silently she passed the letter to Rose, then went down to help in the cafe.

Rose read the letter, but she read between the lines as Holly had not done, and guessed Sam's need for his daughter's love. Oh, Sam, she thought sadly, put her first. Just this once.

Charlotte Saunders smiled a welcome as she opened the door to Celia Hammerton, and showed her into the pretty sitting-room. Celia, was wearing a grey linen dress, relieved only by a scarlet belt and matching clutch bag, Charlotte's cotton skirt and blouse felt girlish by comparison.

They talked casually for a few minutes before Celia came to the point.

'Charlotte, can I ask you something? You won't take offence, think I'm – well – overstepping the mark?'

Charlotte looked away. Was she ready to be questioned about her feelings for Derek Gregson? Did she know enough about them herself? But she knew Celia had come for some answers.

'I won't know until you ask – will I?'

Celia had not got to her present position without plenty of straight speaking, but this was different. This was no hard headed business discussion, this was about herself, her innermost feelings.

'Derek – is there anything between you? Anything I should know?'

Charlotte hesitated. 'Such as?'

'Such as plans for a future together? I know that you are part of his life here.'

'I was once, a big part of his life.' Charlotte spoke slowly, measuring her words. 'I suppose if I had gone to America with him when he asked me we would have built up a good life together. But I was so young, and I had my mother to think of.

'Since he came back, well we've been like two wary swimmers at the edge of the pool. One of us dipping our toes in, then the other. Sometimes we've waded deeper, but always one of us has drawn back – neither of us would commit ourselves.

'But now – well, if he asked me to go back with him this time,' Charlotte hesitated, looking at Celia, knowing how much her answer meant to the other girl. 'I think, no, I know, I would say yes.

'And you, Celia?' Celia looked at her ruefully.

'Until I saw Derek again I would have just said I wanted him as a lover. Someone to be there – sharing, caring, but not the major element in my life. Since I saw him again, well I know now that my feelings are deeper than that, if he asked me to marry him – .'

'And your career?'

'I think Derek would understand about that. He has the same driving force; the desire to win; to come out on top. If not, well I have done some thinking. Derek means more to me than a career. The only thing is. . . .'

Celia looked at Charlotte, and Charlotte saw the uncertainty, the fear.

'What if Derek wants to stay here? In England, near his mother? You would be still in your own world, a world you know, whereas me—'

Charlotte was silent, but her eyes asked the question.

'Oh, yes! I would stay with him. But my life has been New York. America has moulded me, made me what I am. If I stayed here, would I still be myself? The person Derek married?'

Celia's quiet words held a hint of sadness.

'His mother is getting better. Rather reluctantly,' Charlotte smiled. 'Margaret's afraid of being well because she knows it will mean another parting from her son.

'Celia, can I give you some advice? I've known Derek as long as I can remember. Don't rush him, he likes to make his own decisions, direct his own life, and he will shy away from both of us if he feels that we are arranging his life. Let him set the pace.

'But why am I telling you all this?'

Celia smiled.

'Because you are a nice person. I wish you weren't, then I could fight with all I have.

'But Charlotte, if – if Derek does ask me to marry him, will you be my friend?'

'Yes, I'll be your friend,' Charlotte promised. 'Now I

am going to make you a good cup of English tea, and you'll drink it and like it,' she laughed.

In spite of her misgivings the following week was sheer magic for Celia. Derek seemed to have put all his worries, his fears about his mother and for his business, behind him.

They explored the hills and moors of Yorkshire. Celia found a new, unexpected delight in striding beside Derek in unaccustomed flat shoes. She enjoyed his pleasure as he hushed her so that he could point out the wild birds, or as he searched, as he and Charlotte had done years before for a rare flower, almost hidden by the long grass.

She munched sandwiches and drank coffee from a thermos, and lay on the heather, serene and content in his arms.

At night Celia came into her own. Derek took her to the best hotels, theatres, night clubs. But there was no softening in Margaret Gregson's attitude towards her as she watched her son going out night after night. Celia stood for America – and for parting.

But Celia had to return to New York. On their last evening they dined in Scarborough, then Derek parked the car and slipped an anorak of his across Celia's shoulders.

'Come on, we'll stroll. It is a perfect evening.'

They walked along the Spa. The sun was fading, turning the sea, into a shimmering expanse of gold tinted waves; the ripples played soft music on the sandy shore. They sat on the seat by the sea wall, and Derek took her hands in his.

'I shall miss you,' he said gently. And the words which could mean so much or so little, broke the curb

Celia had kept on her feelings.

She was leaving, and all he could say was that he would miss her. She freed her hands and turned to him, throwing caution to the winds.

'And is that all you will do? Are you blind? Don't you see how I feel? I love you! I want to be with you, stay with you. Surely this past week has meant something? Come back with me – or at least ask me to come back to you.'

Her voice broke. Already she had seen the shuttering of Derek's eyes, sensed his withdrawal.

'Celia, this week has been wonderful. My dear, you know I care for you, about you. But you know I have commitments over here—'

'And your commitments in America? Your New York office? Your work? Your flat? You can't keep on running things from here; you said so yourself; you will have to come back. Your mother is almost well and there are places—'

'Don't say any more!' He stood up, pulling Celia with him. 'I will arrange my mother's future, and my own.'

His words carried on the still night, people looked at them and he took her arm, leading her back to the car.

'I'm sorry,' he told her as he sat beside her. 'We mustn't let it end like this.'

He drew her to him, and she didn't resist as his lips found hers. There was a sense of utter desolation deep in her heart. Desolation that she knew would turn to pain —

As the car drew up outside her hotel, she turned to him.

'I wasn't being callous about your mother, Derek.

There's a couple at the hotel, they have been looking round sheltered accommodation and they are so looking forward to it—'

This time he didn't grow angry, he just nodded.

'I know. The doctor has discussed it with Charlotte and me—'

Charlotte and me – the words echoed in her brain as she lay restless through the long night. Tomorrow Derek would take her to the airport. Tomorrow she would be back home – at least there, she could bury herself in work.

The next day traffic held them up as Derek drove to the airport so their parting had to be brief.

'I shouldn't have got so angry last night,' he told her. 'You were right. I will have to come back to New York, if only to wind things up. I honestly don't know when.

'I know Mother can't stay where she is on her own. If we sold the house and found her somewhere suitable the money would give her independence. I will have to talk to her, but not yet, not until she is stronger. This isn't the right time.'

Celia looked up at him, her love clear in her eyes.

'It would be Derek. If you cared enough.'

Long after the plane was out of sight Derek Gregson sat at the wheel of his car. How was it he could be so ruthless in his business dealings and yet so, yes, he had to admit it, weak in dealing with people he cared about?

Both Dr Wade and Charlotte had urged him to talk to his mother, but he was afraid of hurting her, of watching her spirit crumble as he told her they must sell the home she had shared with the only man she had ever cared about.

Holly, preparing for the evening out she had planned to spend with Roger, made sure everything Rose could possibly need while she was alone, was at hand. Rose wouldn't admit her arthritis was troubling her more, but she didn't need to. Holly knew, just as she knew that during the weeks she had spent with Rose, her eyesight had diminished so that even helping in the cafe was becoming too much.

Long after Holly had left Rose sat in the darkening room. Always, from somewhere she had been able to dredge up the courage to face whatever the future held.

Now in a world growing slowly darker, more pain filled, more desolate, she thought of Roger's wish to start a new life with Holly, whose companionship had come to mean so much to her.

Roger too, had noticed the shadows making Holly's eyes appear deep violet. As they sat in the theatre bar, having a coffee before taking their seats, he leaned across and spoke gently.

'What is it, Holly? Something's wrong. Is it anything I've done?'

She shook her head.

'It's Dad! I wrote to him. I said I wouldn't, but I know I'm partly to blame for everything. He said he will come, but he's said that before,' she added bitterly. 'The point is I'm wishing I hadn't written. I don't even know him any more.'

'Our day out tomorrow? Do you want to cancel it?'

Tomorrow was Saturday and Holly had promised to spend it with Roger. Now she looked at him.

'Why should I want that?'

'I thought, well, if you're expecting your father, you might want to be in. I could come for the day. Meet him with you.'

'No, there is no reason for me to stay around. Besides it's all arranged. Marion has got help in the cafe. If he comes, well – he can wait. I've waited long enough!'

'I'm sorry, love.' Roger leaned across and took her hand. 'Holly, you know how I feel, that I want a chance to make up for the past, to build a life together —

'Look love, I've got the chance of a better flat. I've already said yes and plan to decorate it, make it into a home. But it won't be, not without you. Oh, I know what it was like last time, but I'm older now, wiser. I need you, Holly! Give me a chance, please.'

His voice petered out as he met Holly's eyes. They were hidden by the dim light, but he sensed the wariness in their depths, and he saw Holly shake her head.

'I don't know Roger, you must give me time – I said I would think about it. Wait a little longer, please?'

The sound of the bell indicated they must take their seats, but in the brief moments when they had the bar to themselves, Roger drew her to him, brushing her lips with his.

'I do love you, Holly,' he whispered. 'Remember that when you are deciding our future.'

'Auntie Rose, are you sure you will be all right?'

'Of course I will! A full day out will do you the world of good. Get along with you.'

Still Holly hesitated. She dropped on her knees beside Rose's chair, looking up at her. Rose put out her hands and slowly traced the contours of the face of the girl she cared for so deeply. Words trembled on her lips, but she bit them back and smiled.

'Come on now, away with you.'

Only when the sound of the car Roger Johnston had borrowed for the day died away did Rose reach behind the cushion of her chair and pull out a letter.

Reaching for her magnifying glass, slowly, reluctantly, she deciphered the printed words.

It was just after lunch when Marion Formby asked Rose if she would see a visitor. Rose was laying back in her chair. Fearful of the future, she was, as she so often did, reliving memories of the past.

Marion Formby's words broke into her reverie and Rose's thoughts were still hazy as she looked at the tall, shadowy figure standing in the doorway.

The sound of the cafe door opening sent Marion hurrying downstairs before she had chance to say any more and slowly the figure advanced from the shadows into the curtained light of the sitting-room.

Still Rose could not distinguish his features, only when he came over to her chair and spoke her name, 'Rose! Oh, Rose! Don't you know me?' Did recognition sharpen her mind?

'Sam! Sam Webster! It is you — ?'

She couldn't see the expression of disbelief, disbelief that changed to pity as she peered up at him through narrowed eyes.

'Yes, it's me! But surely – you were expecting me? I wrote to Holly. . .'

'Yes, you wrote to Holly, but as for expecting you—'

She didn't say any more, she didn't have to, the implication of her words was there.

Sam was the first to break the silence.

'Holly? She said she was working in the cafe. I didn't see her.'

'She does have some time off! Did you expect her to be sat waiting? Holly's changed, Sam. She's no longer a little girl you can leave for anyone to care for, she's a grown woman – a woman who has already suffered more than she should have—'

She broke off and gestured to her visitor.

'Sit down, Sam. No, not there, sit in the light so that I can see you.' Sam sat down, turning the chair so that he, in his turn, could see Rose.

'Rose, your eyes? Holly didn't say anything.'

'I asked her not to. She's the one who needs help, not me!'

Her voice tailed off, and Sam sat still, recognising perhaps for the first time how much this woman cared for his daughter.

'I want to help—'

Rose turned on him, anger sharpening her voice.

'Do you, Sam? The way you did in the past when Holly needed you?'

'I didn't mean to hurt her.'

'No-one ever does! Roger didn't want to hurt her, you didn't. At least Roger admits to being wrong. You had a grandson – and you never even saw him!

'Have you any idea what Holly went through? Especially when Roger—'

She halted, not sure how much Holly would want her to say. She had already said too much.

'When Roger – what?'

'It was more than he could take, he left her.'

'Typical! I said the marriage was . . .'

'Be quiet, Sam! You don't know the whole story. You weren't there!'

He stood up and crossed to the window.

'Tell me,' he said slowly. 'I need to know.'

'No, Sam. Holly must tell you. Holly and Charlotte.'

'Charlotte?'

'A girl who has been a good friend to your daughter.' A friend thought Rose, who knows something I have not yet learned.

'Rose, have I made another mistake in coming? Should I go away?'

The quiet despair in the man's voice filled the small room, and cut through Rose's hostility.

'No, Sam. You must stay now. See Holly, and talk to her. Let her see that this time at least you came. I can't promise a welcome – the bitterness has gone too deep for that, but you can try.

'She won't be very late.'

'Where has she gone?'

He asked the question diffidently, as though he had already accepted the fact that he had no right to question Holly's whereabouts.

'She's out for the day, with Roger.'

'With Roger? After what happened?'

'As I said, you don't know the whole story. Roger is a decent lad.'

Slowly, painfully, Rose stood up, and as he saw her reach for her sticks he stood beside her.

'Oh Rose, I hate to see you like this! Surely there is something to be done.'

'There might be, some day,' she answered gently. 'Now I'll make some coffee.'

'No, let me—'

'Sit down. I have to move about. Loosen up.'

Before Rose reached the kitchen however, Marion Formby appeared with a tray, which she placed on a long table in front of the settee.

Sam sat beside Rose. Rose picked up the coffee pot. He watched as she ran her fingers over the rim of the cups, as she bent low over the tray to pour.

'How bad?' He had taken her hand, and was waiting for an answer.

'It's bad, Sam! Very bad.' She was silent, remembering the specialist's words spoken all those months before.

– until you have nothing further to lose

Then, the decision had seemed so long away, now—

It would be so easy to turn to Sam, to take the comfort he was holding out, but Holly must come first. She smiled.

'Still black, with two sugars?'

'You remembered?'

Somehow that insignificant detail eased the tension between them. They still had a long way to go before they regained their old friendship but at least conversation flowed easily between them.

Sam talked about his travels, told her about the new possibilities that were unfolding, and when Rose said she wanted to rest, he went downstairs and had a meal in the cafe.

As he ate he thought about his daughter, suddenly aware how much he needed her to become part of his life. But what if he had left it too late? What then?

It was shortly after nine o'clock when Rose and Sam heard the rush of Holly's light footsteps up the stairs.

'I came home early, I was worried about you – '

Her voice broke off as a tall figure rose and looked towards her. Sam took a step forward and held out his hands, but still Holly didn't move.

He was here – the father she had so often needed in the past. She felt a sudden constriction in her throat, the pain of tears behind her eyes. She had an indescribable urge to run to him, to let the years fall away and be held close, comforted as she had been when she was small.

But she mustn't. This man, standing so quietly, waiting, was a stranger, a stranger who had no part in her life —

Ten

Rose White was the first to break the silence.

'I think I'll go to my room now. I'm a bit tired.'

Holly moved then, but Rose waved her away. 'No, Holly! You needn't come. I can manage. Stay and talk to your dad.'

Sam Webster watched as his daughter walked slowly across the room and sank onto a pouffe in front of the fire. As she raised her eyes and looked at him, he made a quick movement towards her.

'Holly, you've changed. You're so like your mother. Oh, Holly, she'd have known what to say. . . .'

He sank into a chair, burying his face in his hands.

'What is there to say? I've grown up, Dad. I've been a wife, and a mother—'

Her voice broke, and Sam looked at her.

'I should have been there love. I know that now.'

'But you weren't!' Holly's words held no condemnation. Her voice was flat, toneless. When she spoke again it became warm with memories.

'He was so beautiful, my Nigel.' For the first time she sat up and looked directly at her father. 'You know, he was a bit like you. I hadn't realised it before, but he was long, and lean, even at his age.'

'Talk to me about him, love,' Sam said gently.

'What is there to say? I wrote to you, but—'

'I was moving about. Your letter didn't catch up with me.'

Even to Sam's ears the words sounded feeble. He hadn't been prepared for this sudden rush of tenderness he felt towards his daughter. In the half light she looked little more than a child herself. He wanted to touch the mop of red gold curls; to draw her to him, to tell her he would always be there if she needed him again.

'Holly, I do understand—'

It was as though he had pressed a switch. Holly's green eyes flashed.

'No you don't! No one does. How can anyone know how it feels to put a warm, living child into his cot; to cuddle him and tuck him up? Listen to him gurgling as you tiptoe out of the room – then, when you go back—'

This time the tears came. Slow, breath-catching sobs, but when Sam walked across and laid a gentle hand on her shoulder, Holly shrugged him off. She knew she was denying herself comfort she badly needed, but the past year had driven a wedge between them.

She stood up, pushing her hair from her face.

'Look, Dad, I'll have to go into Auntie Rose now. I give her a bit of massage, and read to her a while—'
Sam nodded.

'All right, love. I'll go.' But at the door he hesitated. 'I'm taking Rose out for a few hours tomorrow. I thought she might enjoy a drive. Would you come with us, please?'

'Sorry, but I am a working girl. I can't leave Marion without proper help tomorrow.'

Charlotte Saunders let herself into her small terrace home, and sighed as she hung her light jacket away. Much as she enjoyed her work at elderly Dr Wade's surgery she found it tiring on occasions.

Charlotte had a secret feeling that he was looking forward to the day when his old receptionist Beryl returned. Beryl, she was sure, was more tolerant of the old doctor's easy going ways.

She scrambled eggs and curled up in a chair with a tray beside her. Charlotte was restless. The letter with the American post-mark propped beside the clock hadn't helped. It was nearly three weeks since Celia had returned to America. The letter was bright, sparkling with false gaiety. There was no outright mention of Derek Gregson, but her need of him was there in every line.

Charlotte knew the time was coming when she would have to make decisions about her own life. Her extended period of unpaid leave from the health centre in London where she worked was coming to an end, as was her temporary job with Doctor Wade.

But what did she want? She had hardly seen Derek Gregson since Celia's departure. Charlotte had been round to see his mother several times, and Derek had emerged from his study for brief periods, but the old closeness between them seemed to have faded.

She frowned as there was a knock at the door.

'Do I have to throw my hat in?' he grinned.

'Derek! This is nice – want some coffee?'

'No thanks! I drink gallons when I'm working. It will be coming out of my ears soon. Charlotte, I'm sorry I haven't been in touch, but I had a lot of work to bring up to date after Celia left. It's a lot more complicated seeing to things from this end.'

Charlotte nodded.

'There's a jug of lemonade in the fridge.'

'Like your mum's?' he asked, making for the kitchen.

'The same jug, even,' he smiled as he put the old fashioned, flowered jug on the table. 'You know, I used to think your mother's lemonade was the most wonderful taste in the world.'

'And I loved that fizzy stuff out of a bottle you used to have. I thought you must be very rich to buy it, though.'

Suddenly they were laughing together as they had done so often before. He perched on the arm of her chair.

'How's Holly?' he asked.

'Fine, as far as I know. I called at the cafe for tea the last time I was in Scarborough. Her father is staying near for a while, but I haven't met him. He had taken Rose out for a drive.'

Charlotte found her head resting in the crook of Derek's arm, felt his hand close round her own. His fingers gentled her chin, turning her face up to his.

Suddenly his eyes were filled with emotion. 'Charlotte,' he said, charging the word with a deep intensity. 'I—'

Words hovered like a taut wire between them, but the moment was shattered by the ringing of the telephone.

Charlotte replaced the receiver.

'Doctor Wade,' she said quietly, 'couldn't find some papers.'

But the moment had gone. Derek drained his glass and stood up.

'Actually, I have a request from Mum. There are some sheltered homes nearly completed up near Peasholme Park. Would you go with us to view them tomorrow? She wants a female opinion as well as mine.'

'I will if four-thirty isn't too late. I have an afternoon surgery and never quite know what time I'll get away.'

'We'll pick you up, then.' He lingered, his hand on the door knob.

'Charlotte, have dinner with me tonight?'

'Sorry, but I've arranged to go to a concert with some friends. Another time?'

'Another time, then. See you tomorrow.'

Long after he had gone Charlotte stood by the window. Why had she refused an outing she would have enjoyed? It wouldn't have mattered at all if she hadn't shown up for the concert. Was it pique because she had seen so little of him? Or was it something to do with Celia's letter?

The following afternoon was not as busy as Charlotte expected, and by four oclock she was changed and waiting for Derek. She smiled when she heard a car, glad they were early. But it was a tall, slightly round shouldered, scholarly looking man who stood on the step.

'Miss Saunders? I'm Sam Webster, Holly's father. Could I have a few words with you?'

'Well, I am expecting friends, but come in.'

Charlotte felt her words less than cordial, but she remembered how lost and folorn Holly had been. She had needed someone, and neither her father or her husband had been there.

Once inside she waited for Sam to speak.

'Miss Saunders, I want to thank you for what you did for my daughter. I should have been there and I wasn't.' The words were said quietly, a simple statement of fact.

'I want to make up for that, help Holly in any way I can, and I feel there is still something I don't know. Something that might help me to understand. Rose West said you were her first friend in Baynton, that you might help.'

Charlotte turned from him. His keen grey eyes were too observant.

'Leave me alone! I don't deserve to live!' She shivered as she remembered that nightmare climb up the cliff. But that was Holly's secret.

'There's probably very little I can tell you that you don't already know. I met Holly on the beach, the tide was coming in and we both had to scramble up the cliff. We were wet and cold and I took Holly home with me. She had come to see Rose West, who was not at her old address, so I suggested Holly stayed with me until we could locate her.'

She turned and looked at him.

'That's all.'

Their eyes met, and they both knew there was a lot more that could have been said, but Sam Webster just nodded. A car drew up outside and Sam held out his hand.

'Your friends, so I will leave. Thank you again.'

His quiet courtesy made Charlotte a little ashamed. But what else could she have done? She had promised Holly.

The houses were all Margaret Gregson could wish for. A semi-circle of detached bungalows, with a central dining-room and a games room. The warden was young, but obviously capable and fond of her job.

As Margaret and Charlotte stood watching Derek walk over to the sales office Margaret's eyes misted with tears.

'Not long now,' she whispered. 'He'll soon be gone.

'Drop me off at home,' Margaret ordered with a touch of her old bossiness. 'You take Charlotte out to dinner somewhere. I have Annie coming to hear about the houses and have a game of cards.'

'She who must be obeyed,' whispered Derek before he helped his mother out of the car. 'Sit still. I'll be back.'

'Where to now? I'm yours to command!'

'Well, either a pub meal or cold meat and salad at my place?'

'Cold meat and salad,' he answered promptly. 'Hang on another minute, I'll nip back for a bottle of wine.'

They chatted easily as they ate, then Charlotte closed the kitchen door on the dirty dishes, and they sat side by side on the settee.

'Remember what happened the other time I came to dinner? Bill Menzies showed up. Do you ever hear from him?'

'No, there was nothing left to say,' Charlotte answered.

'But how do you feel? Do you—'

'Derek, it doesn't matter. How I feel is my own affair—'

'When it concerns you it is my affair as well. Oh Charlotte.'

Suddenly she was in his arms. His lips were firm on hers and she let her own ardour match his own as her arms closed round his neck, drawing him closer. When they finally drew apart there was a tender smile on his face, and his arms still held her.

'Charlotte, come back to America with me? Please darling. You're good for me. When I'm with you I'm calm, contented. I love you.'

Charlotte loosened his hold and picked up her wineglass, sipping the rich red liquid without even tasting it. She didn't want Derek to see her face, he knew her too well. She didn't want him to know that her whole body ached to turn to him, hold him, tell him she would marry him whenever he wanted.

Carefully she remembered his words, calm, contented. Was that a true basis for marriage? For later years, yes, but now there should be something more. Something vital, alive.

'But is it the right kind of love, Derek?'

'It's a lasting, caring love. Please, I need you. Oh, I know there will be no highlights, but on the other hand there won't be the lows either.'

But highs and lows are part of marriage, thought the girl sitting so quietly beside him.

'I'm sorry, Derek. But it wouldn't work. Oh yes, I do love you, but not enough to go to the other side of the world.' She forced herself to look at him. Forced her eyes not to deny her words. 'Go back to New York,

135

spend some time with Celia, and see how things go. We'll write, keep in touch.'

Long after Derek had gone Charlotte sat, unaware that the room was getting colder, knowing only that she had sent Derek away. Derek whose life she had dreamed of sharing ever since she was a child. What was there left for her now?

'Come outside, love. I've something to show you.'

Holly Johnston stared at her young husband. Puzzled, she followed him out of the cafe and stared.

'How about that then?' Roger said proudly.

Holly walked round the bright yellow three-wheeled car and burst out laughing.

'Oh Roger! Are you really going to drive around in this?'

As he looked at his wife, laughing as she had done during the early days of their marriage, Roger's own heart lightened. Surely if they could still laugh together, there was hope for them.

'I certainly am, and so are you. Now!'

Sam Webster, going into the cafe paused, and looked at the car. Holly turned to him, still laughing.

'Oh Dad! Did you ever see anything like it?'

Sam smiled. It was the first time she had been entirely natural with him.

'I have now,' he said gently. 'Going out?'

'Yes, but Roger won't tell me where,' Holly answered. 'I'd better get a coat.'

The two men stood. It was Roger who spoke first.

'I do love her, Mr Webster. I want to make up to her, to make her happy.'

'We both do, Roger,' the older man said gently. 'But

it isn't always easy to rectify the past.'

Although Roger hadn't said anything, Holly soon guessed their destination. It was an hour and a half later when they drew up in a wide street of terrace houses, on the outskirts of Leeds.

Roger took a key from his pocket, and looked at his wife, his face anxious.

'I was going to decorate, but I thought you'd rather choose the colours. I've given it a good clean.'

The rooms were certainly no luxury abode, but they were large and airy, and Holly knew she could make a comfortable home out of them. Suddenly, unable to bear her silence any longer Roger took hold of her.

'Holly, you have to be fair to us both. We have to try again. We promised, for better or worse, remember. Surely it is time for the better part?'

As she looked up at him, her large green eyes dark pools that gave nothing away, he loosened his hold, cupping her face in his hands, kissing her gently, her eyes, her cheeks, and lastly, her lips.

Holly knew she could not put her decision off any longer.

'Look, Auntie Rose goes for the laser beam on her eye early next Tuesday. I don't want to tell her, not until afterwards. I know she's afraid of what could happen—'

Her voice broke, and instinctively she sought comfort from her husband. His arms tightened, but there was fear in his voice.

'Are you trying to tell me that if – if the operation is not a success, you won't come back to me?'

'Oh no! That wouldn't be fair at all. I'll come Roger, whatever the result, but if the worst happens, I might want a few more days, just to help her. She's been so good to me.'

'As long as I know you are coming soon.'

Again she felt his lips on hers, and this time she put her arms round him and kissed him back. Then she smiled.

'Come on then, if I'm going to make anything of this place we'd better start measuring.'

Sam Webster and Holly Johnston sat alone in the quiet corner of the hospital area. Although the laser-beam treatment for her eye took only a few seconds, there were tests to be done first.

'Dad, I'm so afraid!'

Suddenly it seemed natural to Holly to turn to her father for reassurance. Sam too, felt fear cold inside him, but the fact that his daughter had turned to him, slipped her hand in his, shown him her need, helped him to smile, to slip an arm round her and reassure her.

'It will be all right, love,' he said gently. 'It has to be.'

It was over an hour later when a young nurse led Rose back to where Holly and Sam were waiting.

Rose, her eyes hidden behind dark glasses, managed a smile.

'Let's go home,' she whispered. Sam and Holly each took an arm.

When they reached Rose's sitting-room Sam stood back and it was Holly who guided Rose to her chair.

'I'd been hoping for a miracle.' Holly and her father had to strain to catch the words. 'I'd read about it. People seeing instantly.'

Tears ran down her cheeks. She made no effort to

remove her glasses and wipe them away.

Holly was too upset, too out of her depth to know what to say. Sam went and knelt by her chair.

'What did they say?'

'Just to keep the glasses on in strong light. And not to put any strain on my eyes for a day or two.'

Sam stood up, walked to the window and partly drew the curtains.

'Take your glasses off,' he told her.

Holly halted in the doorway.

Rose said nothing. Her eyes wandered round the room, then rested on Holly.

Suddenly, her voice high-pitched with disbelief, Rose pointed.

'Holly, you're wearing something shiny round your neck. It's blue, like your blouse. And, Sam, your tie is a sort of green!'

'Nearly!' He laughed. 'But Holly's necklace is blue right enough.'

Suddenly the small room, which had been so full of fear, exploded with laughter. Then they were hugging Rose, all three of them with arms entwined.

Holly was the first to break away. As she went into the kitchen, she looked back.

Sam was still there, his hands covering Rose West's. Holly didn't hurry with the tea.

It was late evening. Holly and Rose were listening to soft music on the radio when the telephone rang, Holly knew it was Roger.

'Rose? Oh, Roger, she's so much better. Give her another day or two.'

Then she was silent. Rose couldn't make out the

words drifting down the line, but she knew —.

'Roger, I. . . .' Holly was hesitant, and looked towards Rose. Rose nodded, managing a smile.

'All right.' Holly tried to hide her fears. 'Pick me up on Friday. That will give the new waitress time to settle in.'

Holly went and sat on the pouffe, staring into the flickering flames of the gas fire.

'Holly.' Rose West leaned over. 'You once said if there was anything you could do for me, you would. Now listen. Your happiness is the best present I could have.

'You must give Roger a chance. Don't pretend feelings that aren't there. That wouldn't be fair to either of you. Equally, don't let the past close your heart.

'You loved Roger once and you were happy together, perhaps it is time for us both to take a new look at our lives.'

But that night Holly heard again the crash of the waves as she and Charlotte had struggled round the headland. There were things neither Rose West or Roger had been told.

Holly looked round the flat. She and Roger had been together for five weeks. They had transformed the dingy rooms into a cheerful home. Bright covers and matching curtains blended well with the primrose walls.

Then she heard Roger's key in the door.

'Something smells good.' He smiled as he stooped to kiss her,

After the meal he asked her if she would like to go

anywhere. Mostly their Saturdays had been spent decorating. Now it was done.

'Yes! Will you take me to Baynton?'

'Fancying a chat with Charlotte?'

'No,' Holly's voice was quiet. 'I want to walk on the sands and talk.'

Roger took his wife's hand as they left the car. It was a perfect September day and they soon left the holiday makers behind.

Roger was carrying his anorak. He spread it over a smooth outcrop of rock and they sat side by side.

Holly turned from Roger, gazing out over the sea.

'Roger, you've always sensed I was keeping something back from you, well, you were right.

'After Nigel died, you drifted away from me. I know now it wasn't your fault – or mine. We were just too young.

'There wasn't an hour of the day I didn't think about our baby. His things were still around and I couldn't bear to touch them.

'When you turned on me it seemed like the end of everything. Even so, I was sure you would come back. I made myself tidy the flat and make a meal. I scraped it into the bin.

'You didn't come the next day, or the next. I didn't know that two rooms could be so empty; that two days could have so many hours in them.

'The next morning there was no food in the house. I just made a cup of tea and sat. Then I remembered Auntie Rose. How she used to cuddle me and make things come right. I knew I had to find her.

'I just grabbed what money I had and an old rucksack and went.

'I didn't feel as though it was me travelling. I felt empty. I just wanted someone to care. But she wasn't there. You – Dad – and now Auntie Rose, all gone out of my life.

'I started to walk. Auntie Rose used to bring me here, but she warned me never to come alone, because of the tide. But I just wanted to be somewhere where I'd been happy.

'I sat on the beach. The waves were drifting up so gently. I felt calm as though I had come to the end of all the things that could hurt me. I watched the waves getting nearer and thought, *if I just sit here nothing will ever hurt again*.

'I heard a shout, but ignored it. Then a stone and a clump of earth landed near me. I looked up and there was someone on the cliff, but she could have nothing to do with me. No one was going to enter my lovely dream world.

'Then there was someone beside me, shaking me. I tried to make her go away, but she just yelled at me to move.

'I didn't care – until the waves broke round our ankles. The water was cold, frightening. Suddenly I realised I wasn't ready to die.'

She looked up at Roger. His eyes were misted with tears.

'The next hour is just a blur. Somehow Charlotte got me round the headland and up the cliff. Then she took me to her home – the rest you know.'

Roger took her in his arms, cradling her tenderly.

'Oh, darling, I'm so sorry. I just couldn't carry your hurt as well as mine. But we can put it behind us, start again. I'll help you forget. I love you so much.'

'I know, but there can't be any going back. I've tried so hard, but the past is always there. I do care about you, Roger, I always will, but it's not the same as when we started out together.

'I have to make my own future, in my own way.'

Her eyes filled with a sadness no nineteen-year-old should know.

Roger kissed her, so very gently, then drew her to her feet.

'Come on, love. We'd better get back.'

Mundane words, ordinary words that concealed his heartbreak.

When they were within sight of the town he drew her into a small, sheltered alcove in the beach gardens.

'Thank you for telling me,' he said quietly. 'Holly, I have something for you. I've had it a long time, but never felt able to give it to you.

'Now I know there are no more secrets between us, I want you to have it. I've carried it around for ages,' he apologised as she removed the scruffy wrapping.

'Roger!' Her voice held utter disbelief as she opened the small silver locket and looked down at the face of baby Nigel.

'A friend took it in the flat, but afterwards, well, he didn't like to send it. When I was leaving I called round for it. I wasn't sure, but I thought—'

'It's the best present I could have had. I've been so worried I would forget what he looked like, now he'll always be with me.'

She was crying now, soft, gentle tears that would wash away pain.

Roger held her, but his heart was heavy. He knew her tears meant she was ready to start that new life she had talked about. A life in which he had no part, except as a friend.

As Holly and Roger set off on their walk on Baynton beach, Derek and his mother were saying goodbye. The sale of Margaret Gregson's house had gone through with amazing ease.

The sale had resulted in a nice little nest-egg for Margaret. The warden of the sheltered housing was kind and efficient. Derek knew he could return to New York with an easy mind.

But he still hated leaving her.

'Won't you change your mind, Mother, and come to the airport? Charlotte would bring you home before she returns the hired car.'

'No, love, I don't want any more public goodbyes.'

'Oh, Mum, it won't be like last time. I'm going back to a thriving business. I can take a holiday whenever I like. I won't stay away as long as last time. Only don't get ill again.'

'Stop fussing,' Margaret said gently. 'I've learned my lesson. And you don't have to come, not if there are more important things to do.'

'There won't be,' he assured her firmly, as he held her close.

'Now I must go. Charlotte will be waiting.'

Charlotte slipped into the car beside Derek. He reached out and touched her cheek, so gently.

'Another goodbye,' he said softly.

Charlotte smiled. He drove smoothly away.

There was an ache in Charlotte's heart as she saw the brown tinged leaves, and the gardens rich with Michaelmas daisies. An ache not only for the passing of her summer at home, but for the parting soon to come.

They stood looking at the planes on the runway, and the minutes ticked slowly away. When the flight number was called Derek turned and held her close.

'You do know that if ever you need me. . . .'

Charlotte silenced him.

'Hush, we both know that. Now go back to New York; to the life you love – and to Celia,'she added almost silently.

Almost before she knew it Derek was down below, waving. Charlotte lifted her hand in response. She was glad he was too far away to see her eyes.

She had one last thing to do. Her fingers were surprisingly steady as she took Celia's letter from her bag and dialled the number.

She didn't worry about the time difference. Celia wouldn't mind being disturbed. Not when she knew Derek was on his way to New York.

When she got home, the house seemed cold and unfriendly, as though it knew she was turning her back on it. Soon a friend of hers would be starting her married life in the little terrace house.

She went to bed early. But tossed restlessly, troubled by thoughts of all that had happened.

Strangely enough it was Bill who strayed mostly into her mind. Bill, with whom she had shared a few brief days in the spring. Now it was autumn. Who was there to share that with?

Eleven

Like most other people, Bill Menzies, in spite of new technology, hated visiting the dentist. After two sleepless nights, however, he found himself sitting in a small waiting room waiting his turn.

There were only two empty seats, one next to him, one in the opposite corner. When the door opened to admit a formidable figure of a woman, who looked round with a steely look in her eye, Bill grabbed the first magazine he could and stared at it intently, breathing an almost audible sigh of relief as the newcomer took the chair opposite and immediately began a description of her intense suffering to her luckless neighbour.

Bill turned the glossy pages, not really interested, then suddenly the grating voice of the newcomer, the antiseptic smell of the waiting room, faded. He stared at the photograph; not a very big one, after all an up and coming fashion buyer meeting an up and coming business man off a plane at Kennedy Airport is not the news of the year, but adequate to fill the odd corner.

To Bill it like tearing open a newly healed wound.

What was Celia Hammerton doing meeting Derek Gregson? Bill had been so sure Charlotte would be returning to New York as the wife of her old childhood friend, but there was no mention of her in the brief caption. He glanced back at the date; September; the magazine was two months old.

Vaguely he became aware of the receptionist repeating his name, and the stares of the other patients. His nervousness had vanished. He strode into the surgery anxious only to get the treatment over.

Bill didn't give a thought to the work that had been getting on top of him during his spell of toothache, or the meeting of the Park Superintendents that he was supposed to attend, his mind had only one thought – where was Charlotte?

There was a pay phone opposite. He went across and dialled the Baynton number that still lingered in his mind, but it was a stranger who answered.

'Charlotte Saunders? Sorry, but Charlotte returned to London six weeks ago now. I am in touch, though. Could I give her a message?'

'No, no thank you. Sorry to have troubled you.'

Bill walked to the car. So Charlotte was back in London, probably in her old job and her old flat. For the first time he thought of what he would have said to her if she had been in Baynton. No, he had to see her. Telephones were too impersonal. He needed to see her eyes when they met, to hear every inflection in her voice —

The November evening was damp and dark when he drove out and parked near the Health Centre. He knew Charlotte's hours were unpredictable, that she sometimes worked in the evening, but he had to wait.

His attention was fixed on the people leaving the building. Charlotte was almost level with the car when he saw her walking towards the entrance.

She had paused under a street lamp, looking in her bag. The pale light illuminated strands of dark hair escaping from her rain hood, added a fairy touch to the mist drops on her blue shiny raincoat.

He opened the car door and the noise disturbed her.

'Charlotte!'

He walked towards her, and saw the dawn of wondering disbelief in her brown eyes, the way her arms went out towards him, then dropped back to her sides.

'Bill!'

They stood facing each other, neither daring to make a move. Then Bill found his voice.

'I only knew today, that Derek had gone back to America. Charlotte, I'm so sorry if it made you unhappy? If Derek—'

Charlotte was shaking her head.

'Derek went with my blessing. I'm glad he's happy. But you? I didn't expect. . . .'

Her voice tailed off and Bill took one of her hands. It was cold and damp and he covered it with both his own.

'You should be wearing gloves,' he told her, then they both smiled at the incongruity of his remark. So much on their minds and he talked of gloves.

The little incident lightened the tension.

'Charlotte, we have to talk. Can I take you out or run you home?

'Sorry, but I'm just going in to do an evening clinic.'

'I can wait.'

She shook her head.

'I'll be too tired to talk, to think clearly. The authorities lay a taxi on for us when we work late.'

'Tomorrow then?' But Charlotte's brain was working again.

'Is there any point? Don't you think we said enough that last evening?'

'I said too much,' Bill told her earnestly. 'I want to apologise, to —

'Oh, Charlotte, I want to make a fresh start, to try again. You've been in my thoughts all the time, even though I did think you would be married to Derek. Please, meet me tomorrow. If you don't want to see me any more then, well I'll accept your decision.'

Charlotte, so aware of Bill's hands holding her own, so aware of the pounding of her own heart, hesitated. She had been hurt before, but the wounds were beginning to heal, she was building up a new life for herself, concentrating on her career. But time was passing, the evening patients would soon be arriving, so she nodded.

'Pick me up at my flat about eight oclock. I must go now.'

Bill took Charlotte to the same hotel they had visited the night after Dr Wade's telephone call. The call that had so dramatically altered so many lives.

After the meal they sat in front of a log fire, drinking coffee, and they talked. Bill told her how he had felt his hopes of happiness slipping away during the weekend in Baynton. Told how up to meeting Charlotte, the land had been his only interest, his thoughts only of the beauty he could raise from the richness of the soil.

Charlotte admitted he had been partly right. She had given too much of her time and thoughts to other people's problems, but defended herself, saying again that she could never turn her back on anyone needing help.

'I know that now,' Bill told her. 'I know that I was wrong, but please, can we make a fresh start?'

Charlotte didn't answer. Instead she told him about the happenings in Baynton, about Holly and Roger; about Margaret Gregson's recovery and her new flat; and Bill Menzies let her talk.

When at last they rose to go, Charlotte looked out over the garden.

'Remember the last time,' she asked. 'The lovely spring flowers?'

Once they were wrapped up, Bill took her arm and led her outside. The evening was moonlight sharp, the bare branches stark against the sky, the leaves rustled as they walked. The flower beds were almost bare, waiting for the loveliness that would be spring, but the hedgerows were bordered by straggling Michaelmas Daisies and clumpy, overgrown clusters of chrysanthemums.

'I remember,' he told her, drawing her into his arms. 'But spring will come again. Can we, Charlotte? Can we pretend I didn't say those things? Start again?'

Charlotte looked up at him. In the evening light it was difficult to read his eyes but his voice rang with sincerity, and she nodded.

'It was me as well,' she assured him. 'I should have talked more, explained things better. Hello again, Bill Menzies.'

His kiss was light, gentle, there was plenty of time – now.

Charlotte looked round her flat with satisfaction. The Christmas trimmings were just right. A small tree Bill had brought her fresh from the forest. Bill had reached up and fixed a few tasteful streamers, and the holly he had brought was heavy with berries.

They had talked of going to Baynton, but, although their new home was getting near completion, the young couple were still in Charlotte's house. Holly Johnston and Rose West were going down to Holly's father's home in Hemel Hempstead for Christmas, and Margaret Gregson was full of the festivities that were to take place in the pleasant complex that was now her home.

So they had settled for a small hotel near Windermere. Christmas Day falling on a Monday meant a nice long week-end. Their walking boots were already in Bill's car, Charlotte knew in her heart it was going to be a very special Christmas.

And it was. They spent the day tramping the countryside. They gloried in the solitude; the wide sweeping views; the oneness with the universe that only comes when you leave the cars and the bustle far behind. One day there was a snow flurry and the soft white flakes seemed to wrap them in a world of their own, a world that was becoming dearer with every hour they spent together.

At night they became civilised, Charlotte saw a new Bill as he emerged immaculate in his evening suit. She in her turn was well rewarded for the hours she had spent going round the dress shops, when she saw the admiration in his eyes and listened to his whispered compliments.

On the last day they visited an old antique jewellers. Rubies and diamonds sparkled on Charlotte's finger as they danced the evening away.

'Charlotte, dear girl. Do you have to go to Yorkshire a whole three weeks before the wedding?' Bill Menzies pleaded.

'We've been through all this and the answer is yes! Weddings aren't arranged by remote control. Now are you sure you don't want me to see to the flowers?'

'Definitely not! That at least I can do, and yes, I know all the instructions,' he laughed. 'Flowers to decorate the church two days before the wedding, buttonholes and the bride's bouquet when I come.'

Then doors were being slammed. Charlotte hung out of the window as Bill pushed magazines and chocolate into her arms, and then she was away, rushing through the familiar countryside on her way to Yorkshire.

Charlotte looked down at the ruby and diamond ring; now, at last she had found the happiness she thought had eluded her.

The next three weeks flew by. Charlotte shopped for dresses, visited old friends, and almost before she knew it she was helping to unpack boxes of damp, sweet smelling flowers to decorate the old grey church where she would begin her life as Bill Menzies' wife.

It was the evening before her wedding. Charlotte was now regretting her decision to have her night out with the girls the previous evening. With all the preparations almost complete, the hours seemed to

The Love They Once Shared

drag. Then suddenly Holly was there.

'Surprise, surprise!' she laughed. 'I wondered if the bride would like company for her last night?'

'Indeed she would,' Charlotte told her. 'Oh, Holly you do look well, so different from—'

She didn't say the bedraggled object I rescued from the beach, but the thought was in both their minds.

'Things are working out for you?' Charlotte asked as they settled down together.

'Yes, I think I know now where I am going,' Holly said quietly. 'I am pretty certain to get my A levels, then I will start training as a masseuse.'

'And Roger? No regrets?'

'No. A little sadness about what might have been, but so much had come between us. I think Roger realised that, even before I put it into words.

'We shall meet as friends after a while, and I think, no, I know, that if either of us have a second chance of happiness we will both have learned a valuable lesson and not throw it away again.'

'Your father? Will he get here for tomorrow?'

'He said he would, but I wouldn't count on it, he was in Turkey the last time I heard from him. Preparing more magazine articles,' Holly grinned.

'You don't mind then? Once you would have resented him not turning up, not being there to see his daughter in her role as bridesmaid.'

'Yes, but I've grown up a bit more now. Auntie Rose has taught me a lot. I know now that you have to care for people as they are, not as you wish them to be. Dad and I are a lot closer now.

'Anyway, think we can start on some of those nibbles I saw in the kitchen? You decide what we can have and I'll put the kettle on.'

'Kettle be blowed! It's my wedding day tomorrow, remember? The least we can do is open the sherry bottle.'

Later Charlotte went into Holly's room and hugged her.

'I'm so glad you came,' she told her. 'You know that first night, I felt you could be the sister I never had. I still feel that way and there will always be room in my life for you. Don't let's drift apart, we've been through too much together to allow that to happen.'

Charlotte Saunders's wedding day dawned clear and bright. The bride scorned breakfast in bed so the two girls went for a brisk walk on the cliffs, returning just as the flowers arrived.

Charlotte's bouquet was a mass of spring blooms, tastefully arranged among trailing fern. Her eyes were soft as she took out a small card.

A breath of spring for my lovely bride.

Smiling, she opened a drawer and put it with another card bearing almost the same words. A card a little worn at the edges, but still to be treasured. Then she went upstairs to dress.

Inevitably her thoughts turned to Derek and Celia. Would theirs be the next marriage? The thought no longer hurt. Celia had sent a wedding present. A beautiful diaphanous silk shawl. The card had been from both of them.

She was ready in good time. Her dress of cream satin added a glow to her slight suntan. Holly had arranged her hair and her head-dress of tinted orange blossom and pearls lay waiting to be pinned into place.

Doctor Wade was giving her away and when the bell rang Charlotte was glad he was early. He was not very time conscious.

Suddenly she was being hugged until she feared for the delicate trimming on her dress.

'Derek! But how—'

'If you think I am going to allow someone else to give my old playmate away, you are very much mistaken. Oh, it's all right. Mother and Doctor Wade were in the know, but I wanted to give you a surprise.'

'Oh, Derek. You couldn't have given me a nicer wedding present. This makes everything perfect. I didn't know I could be so happy.'

'Talking of wedding presents – you'd better see if this is still in one piece.'

This turned out to be a lovely bone china ornament. A boy and a girl, she with her arms outstretched to catch the red ball the boy was about to throw.

'Derek,' Charlotte felt tears prick as she realised how he must have sought for this particular present. 'It's perfect.'

Then Derek turned to the lovely auburn-haired girl standing by the fireplace.

'Holly,' he said quietly. 'You're beautiful.'

She was. Her dress over the stiffened underslip ranged from deep orange swirling round her calves, to a pale gold, accentuating her slim figure and reflecting orange flecks in her green eyes. Her only jewellery was a silver locket on a slender chain. Her posy of sweet scented violets was edged with tiny golden rosebuds reflecting the colour of her dress.

Derek's eyes met those of Charlotte's. He didn't say you've done a good job. The message was there and as

Charlotte sat for Holly to arrange her head-dress she said a quiet prayer of thanks that she had been in the right place when Holly needed help so desperately.

Alone in Margaret Gregson's flat, Celia Hammerton and Margaret were getting ready for the wedding.

'Please, your hair. Will you let me arrange it for you?'

Margaret was about to retort that her hair had been done the previous day, but bit the words back. She hadn't missed the nervous tremor in Celia's voice. Celia could never take the place of the daughter-in-law Margaret had hoped for, but she was Derek's choice, so she nodded, and thanked her.

When Celia told her they would probably be married in New York later in the year, the elderly lady felt an ache in her heart, but Celia assured her they would come to Baynton for a church blessing, and a mother's blessing too, she added gently.

Margaret patted her hand.

'You will have that,' she said without hesitation.

Then she was ready. Together they left the house for the church, Margaret knew she would pray not only for the couple who were to make their vows but for her son's future with this girl beside her.

Rose West too, was preparing for the wedding. Her heart was thankful as she outlined her mouth with a steady hand. Putting on lipstick was a simple act most women took for granted, but not Rose. The days when she had been unable to see to do things for herself were not too far away for her to remember.

Life had treated Rose kindly over the last few months. Her hands had responded to treatment, she

156

was nearing the top of the list for a hip operation.

Realising she had plenty of time, Rose sat down to wait for Marion Formby. The reception was to be held here at 'Elmtree Cafe,' so Marion was busy.

Rose had enjoyed having Holly back to live with her. Holly had told her father and Rose about the day on the beach. She had told them quietly, without dramatising the scene, but both the older people had been horrified. Sam had held Rose as she wept out her feeling of guilt.

'If I'd kept in touch. I was always going to write, but I let other things—'

'Rose, it wasn't your fault. If it was anyone's it was mine, her father's. I should have been there. But it is too late for regrets. We must build on the future now.'

Their shared guilt had brought them closer together. They had all had a lovely Christmas, and Rose, although she knew Sam would never lose the wanderlust and his thirst for travel, had dared to hope things would be different. He had kept in touch, but now – he had promised to be there for the wedding.

The church was full. Rose, sitting beside Marion, smiled at Margaret Gregson and Celia Hammerton, then looked up as a tall, grey haired man slipped into the pew beside her.

'I told you,' he whispered. 'No more broken promises.

Then the soft strains of the organ began. They stood up and when Sam took her hand Rose didn't draw it away. Slowly they turned.

The bride, leaning on the arm of her childhood friend, looked radiant. Holly had a special smile for the two people she loved. Bill stepped forward, eyes only for Charlotte, and the service began.

Bride and groom made their responses clearly, their voices carrying to every part of the church. Then Bill was kissing his bride and the words of the beautiful wedding hymn,

'Love divine, all love excelling'

rang out as the congregation joined in the singing.

All hearts were full. Laughter and light hearted banter would follow –

Charlotte's house would be sold and her home would no longer be in Baynton, but she would return. The small town that had been the scene of childhood happiness; adult grief and now the most wonderful moments of her life would always have a special place in her heart.